"*Edna and Luna* is a delight from first sentence to last. One can't help but love both *Edna and Luna* for all their flaws and quirkiness as well as the tremendous courage it takes to simply navigate the challenges we encounter on this earth. There's humour here, surprising, delicious observations and comments, curious asides; *Edna and Luna* is feminist, yet never formulaic, and each sentence is precise, luminous. Power's ability to create character, and her command of detail is truly impressive. This is a book where place is both specific and universal—details unique to Phoenix, but with a physicality and relationship to place and circumstance that belongs to us all. There's tenderness, redemption, and wisdom in this book—a simple, quiet, credible healing: what we can give to each other if we would. Powers creates a world you want to stay in, characters you wish you were meeting in your own supermarket, characters you wish were knocking at your door." CAROL POTTER, AUTHOR OF SOME SLOW BEES

"From a crabby widow who runs over people's toes with her grocery cart to a woman who chooses fruit by its vibration, *Edna and Luna* reminds us that family can be found in the most unlikely people. The developing bond and each woman's curious background definitely make the book difficult to put down." TAMMY GONZALES, ASSOCIATE EDITOR, SOUTHWESTERN AMERICAN LITERATURE

"Brilliantly observed and poignantly funny, Edna and Luna is the story of two women—a widow and a New Age healer—whose buried pasts and uncertain futures leave them to discover the complexities of love, the gifts of friendship, and, ultimately, the joys of redemption." MARYLEE MACDONALD, AUTHOR OF BONDS OF LOVE AND BLOOD AND MONTPELIER TOMORROW

"Every sentence bursts with something to be moved by, or marvel at. Two very different women form an improbable friendship: each wants something different out of life; yet through one another, against often absurd odds and never quite in the ways they'd hoped for, each gets what she wants. The southwest of Gleah Powers is particularly akin to the deep south of Flannery O'Connor. Her vision is comic, tragic then comic again in wonderfully truthful, unpredictable twists. Despite taking place in the here and now, we're steeped in a timeless, off-road America where spiritual self-search is acted out in primal, private, highly individual ways, unfiltered by the homogenized fashions and distractions of the so-called larger world." F.X. FEENEY, CRITIC, *LA REVIEW OF BOOKS*, AUTHOR, *ORSON WELLES: POWER, HEART & SOUL*

"A magical odyssey, both internal and external, through the American Southwest as sculpted by Gleah Powers. You will not soon forget either Edna or Luna." JILLIAN LAUREN, NY TIMES BESTSELLING AUTHOR OF *SOME GIRLS: MY LIFE IN A HAREM*

"Gleah Powers has an uncanny ability to capture the real, the religious, the natural, and the absurd that is the Southwest into prose. In this novella, she has reached new heights in portraying characters that are perfectly flawed living in a sprawling city amidst an unforgiving, yet magical, Sonoran Desert. *Edna and Luna*, in the end, is an oasis for the human soul." JOHN M. GIST, FOUNDING EDITOR, *RED SAVINA REVIEW*

"I fell in love with this novella from the very first sentence. Gleah Powers is an angelic writer, telling the vast, wild story of *Edna and Luna* with startling economy, sharp tenderness, and searing wit. This is an essential book to guide us through these uncertain times." ALISTAIR MCCARTNEY, AUTHOR OF *THE END OF THE WORLD BOOK*

"A wonderfully moving and insightful story about loss, healing, redemption, and friendship that pierces the heart. Gleah Powers has written a beautiful novella." LEONARD CHANG, AUTHOR OF *TRIPLINES*

"Gleah Powers is a prose stylist with a gift for conciseness and clarity. Using a well-crafted mix of subtle humour and dramatic tension, she takes the reader through a loving journey of loss, loneliness, ageing, and fulfilment. Meeting *Edna and Luna* is a literary delight." PHIL RICE, AUTHOR OF *WINTER SUN: A MEMOIR OF LOVE AND HOSPICE*

About the Author

Born in Chicago and raised and educated in the American Southwest, Gleah Powers has led a life by turns grounded and nomadic—a perfect preparation for discovering in herself the voices of Edna and Luna. In her early teens, she lived with her grandmother in Phoenix. At 18, she travelled with the production of Michelangelo Antonioni's Zabriskie Point. (Antonioni, suffering from insomnia, liked that Gleah was a worthy opponent at cards. She even taught him to play gin rummy.) Thereafter she studied art in Mexico City and at Cal Arts in Los Angeles; moved to New York where she worked as an actor, model, bartender and administrative assistant to a wealthy philanthropist; and became an explorer and teacher of alternative therapies. These adventures will be detailed in the memoir she is currently writing. *Edna and Luna* is her first novel.

Visit her website: *www.gleahpowers.com*

Edna and Luna
Copyright © 2016 Gleah Powers
All rights reserved.

Print Edition
ISBN: 978-1-925417-18-0
Published by Vine Leaves Press 2016
Melbourne, Victoria, Australia

This is a work of fiction. Any similarity between the characters and situations within its pages and places or persons, living or dead, is unintentional and coincidental.

Cover design by Jessica Bell
Interior design by Amie McCracken

National Library of Australia Cataloguing-in-Publication entry (pbk)
Author: Powers, Gleah, author
Title: Edna and luna / Gleah Powers.
ISBN: 9781925417180 (paperback)
Subjects: Healers--Fiction.
Friendship--Fiction.
Dewey Number: 823.92

edna & luna

Gleah Powers

Vine Leaves Press
Melbourne, Vic, Australia

"Everyone comes into this world with their head between a woman's legs. Think about that."
—Luna McLaren to Edna Harwood

1

In the meat section of Bayless market, Edna Harwood picked up a shrink-wrapped New York steak; and her uterus cramped. Except she wasn't sure exactly where her uterus was. She thought the pain could be coming from the bottom of her stomach or her intestines. The aching reminded her of how it had felt years ago when she'd had a miscarriage. The doctor assured her it wasn't her fault and she should try again. "Nature knows best," he'd said. "It might have been deformed." That was the only time she'd been a patient in a hospital. No matter what the doctor said, she felt that somehow she'd been the cause. She knew it was irrational but for months afterwards, whenever she left the house to take a walk, shop or drive to an appointment, she'd find herself looking over her shoulder as if someone was following her with the intention to punish or maybe even kill her.

Edna never had another pregnancy.

Now, she knew she'd reached the age when the body began to go awry, or as Hank used to say, "the wheels begin to come off," but she would rather die than be alone with some horrible disease. If she lived a long time, she hoped she'd be like her Aunt Clara, who up until her death at ninety-two, still played eighteen holes of golf and drove a car. That would be another twenty-two years. Edna wasn't sure if she had enough money to live that long. She'd have to remember to ask Tom at the Goldwater bank.

She leaned her hips against the meat counter. The coolness seeped through the thin cotton fabric of her slacks. Recalling an article she'd read in *Reader's Digest* about how to breathe to relieve anxiety and pain, she took a deep breath, exhaled slowly through her mouth. Ordinarily, Edna didn't go in for that kind of thing. She thought the idea was too simplistic, a bunch of crap really, but she had nothing to lose.

She did three more rounds of breath and it seemed to help. She wished she'd known about the breathing technique the day, a week after Hank died, when her heart raced so fast the blood pounded hard through the veins in her arms. She thought the bones would burst and she'd become armless, incapacitated like her mother at the end: fed, bathed and wiped at the mercy of a Filipina caregiver named Raquel, who drew thick auburn-coloured, badly shaped eyebrows on her mother's face every morning. Edna's heart wouldn't calm down, so for the first time in her life, she called 911. Five men showed up in two fire engines, lights flashing, sirens screaming at 5:30 in the morning. She didn't want to go to the hospital alone, but there was no one to call. The ER doctor told her she was having an anxiety attack and sent her home with a prescription for Valium.

Now in the market, Edna examined the steak, frowned at the weight and price, and remembered that Hank had been dead for exactly six and a half months. She regretted, yet again, blurting out to his corpse lying in St. Joe's Hospital, before she'd had time to think, "How could you do this to me?" It had been Hank's idea to retire in the heat. They'd lived together in their newly built Phoenix house for only three months. Now she was completely alone in a new city.

Edna called the local Masonic headquarters as Hank had instructed her to do when he died. A group of them came to the hospital. They dressed him in a ceremonial apron; black tasselled red hat and gold Scottish rite ring with the sickle and hammer symbol. After Edna left the room they performed their secret death ritual. She didn't know why they bothered to dress him up. They knew he wanted to be cremated. Edna hoped Hank hadn't heard her outburst.

With Hank's passing, Edna began having flashbacks, images, waves of grief and anxiety about her own death, how she would die—stroke, heart attack? Would she become incapacitated? When would it happen? Who, if anyone, would be there? She remembered the death of her father; she was only thirteen. She suspected he wasn't her real father, but she'd loved him. She grieved once again for her miscarried baby and her pets: three cats and two dogs in total, and the twenty-five little mink from her father's mink farm. She'd named them all when they were born, finger-length babies. Manny had been her favourite. They died with her father in the car accident. He'd been transporting them for slaughter from New Castle, Pennsylvania where they lived on a farm, to a buyer in Pittsburg who said he'd take care of things. Edna's father loved his animals. He'd hold them with a gloved arm and blow into their silky fur. He would have made more money if he could have snapped their necks or at least been able to poison them himself.

Edna relived the death of her mother who at the end said, "I've been a nice person, haven't I? Why is this happening to me?" Bess hadn't been a nice person. She beat her daughter for years. So Edna didn't know how to respond. She became tongue-tied. The one time Bess wanted to be close to her daughter, she was dying. Weak and frail, she gripped Edna's hand so tight neither of them could breathe. She tried to pull Edna into bed. "Lie down with me," she said.

Sometimes, Edna thought she should have tried harder to put everything aside and give her mother the equivalent of an emotional last meal.

Now, she laid the steak back on top of the neatly stacked slabs. Hank was the one who'd loved a good piece of meat. When they first got married, every market had a butcher. Nothing was shrink-wrapped and you could see both sides of a filet mignon, a New York strip, or a rib eye.

She wheeled her cart to the chicken cooler and after scrutinizing the size, weight, date and price, chose a three-pack of breasts. She shivered and buttoned up her cardigan, fingering the Christmas tree pin embedded with tiny emeralds and rubies, a birthday gift from Hank that anchored over her heart. Once Edna pinned something to a garment she tended to leave it there. The temperature outside was a hundred and ten degrees, but the air conditioning in Phoenix was so cold that on her weekly outing to the market and Rose's Beauty Shop, when she drove her Cadillac four blocks to the strip mall on the corner of Bethany Home Road and Seventh Avenue, she had to remember to take a sweater.

Edna carried a sturdy white handbag with a noisy gold clasp that hung from a strap too short for her shoulder and too long for her wrist in the crook of her arm. She had a black one for what passed as wintertime in Phoenix. She'd had fifty pocketbooks back in Chicago with hats to match. Hats with veils and feathers and little gold chains that hung slightly over her eye. But that was when Hank was alive and there were places to go that required a hat.

Edna patted her head as she made her way to Liquor. Her pin curls weren't dry yet. She liked to enhance the natural wave in her hair so she didn't use rollers. As usual, she'd gone to Rose's, before doing her marketing, for her weekly wash and pin curl set—once a month she had a cut and colour ("Sun Kissed Auburn"). When Edna and Hank first moved to Phoenix, Rose had been their cleaning woman. Hank paid the final year of her tuition to beauty school, he was generous like that, and gave her enough money to open her own shop after she graduated. Now all of Edna's services were free of charge.

Edna found it claustrophobic to sit under a dryer. She tied her ocean blue Hawaiian Islands scarf over her wet pin curls, gave Rose a tip and walked to the supermarket. She used to go back and have Rose comb out her hair, but it was so hot in the summertime her frozen food would melt in the car. Rose taught Edna how to brush out her hair at home and use styling gel to hold the waves in place, but Edna rarely bothered anymore.

Rose turned out to be the only one Edna had to talk to after Hank's death. Minutes after he passed, Edna spoke to Mildred, her best friend in Chicago. But after the funeral when she felt so lonely she thought she might disappear, Mildred didn't return her calls. Rose told Edna this was a common occurrence. "Death. Too close," she said.

Edna tried to talk to Fermin, her gardener, Rose's older cousin. He would listen, shake his head, say, "*Ay, pobrecita,*" and gaze at her with empathy in his dark eyes. He understood more English than he could speak. He told Edna stories about when he was a young man; how for days he ran from Immigration, crawled under fences as the desert floor chewed up his belly, all the way from Oaxaca, leaving his family behind. He recounted these stories so often Edna began to understand some Spanish words like *miedo*, *dolor* and *corazón*. Fermin said them with *lágrimas* in his eyes. After he mowed the lawn, before he tended the roses, Edna brought him a beer and they stood there, talking; she with her hands on her hips, Fermin leaning his elbows on the lawn-mower, the sweet smell of freshly-cut grass enveloping them.

One morning, a few weeks after Hank died, Edna woke with an image of herself inhaling gas, her head inside the pink enamel oven that matched the refrigerator and kitchen cabinets. She didn't know if this was still a viable form of suicide, but she couldn't get rid of the thought so she drove to the beauty shop. Rose unlocked the door. Her square body was covered in a plastic cape, and pale green curlers stuck out from her head. "I can't believe he's gone, Rosie." Edna hadn't called her by that name before. Rose spread her arms wide. Edna tried to hold back but she couldn't help herself. She let Rose hold her and rub her back while she sobbed. Later, she felt embarrassed and didn't go back to the shop for a month. She was afraid to try a new place and if she could have lived with grey hair, she might never have gone back.

Now, it was comfort enough when Rose asked "*Como estas, Señora* Harwood? Is it getting easier to live without *Señor* Hank?" Edna would answer, "I'm fine, Rose," and wonder if she'd ever be fine again. She'd close her eyes and try to relax as pungent solutions wafted around her, dryers hummed and scissors snipped. Women, lined up in plastic capes like a flock of blackbirds, some yellow-headed and speaking Spanish, gossiped about husbands, children and in-laws.

One day Rose said, "They have many pills for depression, *Señora*. It happens with widows. They let themselves go and before they know it they have faded away. *Muy malo*. We do not want that, *Señora*."

Maybe I do, thought Edna.

She caught the other women staring at her. Did they think she'd gone downhill? Was it pity or judgment she saw in their eyes? She couldn't tell the difference anymore.

Did they see something in her clothes or demeanour that gave them the impression she was depressed? She made sure to floss her teeth and put on lipstick before she left the house. Sometimes, she did pin together a waistband that had gotten too tight and popped a button. Edna hadn't bought new underwear in a long time, but no one could see that. She'd have to check herself more carefully before she went out.

Edna resented the obligation to keep up appearances and reverted back to her New Castle farm girl roots. Now that Hank was gone and beauty had left her, she felt the freedom, at least around the house, to wear un-ironed, baggy shorts and a cheap sleep bra purchased at the drug store, made by a company she'd never heard of. She began to let the suck out of her stomach, slouched her back and shoulders when she felt like it. Sometimes in the morning, not fully awake, Edna could conjure up the smell of hay and the feeling of space in her body that matched the gently rolling farm hills stretching like waves into the western Pennsylvania skyline.

Luna McLaren arrived in Phoenix with her dog Tula, a half-breed Australian Shepherd with one blue eye, one brown; her belongings in a U-Haul trailer hitched to the back of her ten-year-old Honda station wagon; and the name and address of a man named Darryl written on the back of a faded fortune cookie prediction in her purse. She could still make out the words, "beloved and Rumi."

Darryl ran the Papago Trailer Park on McDowell Road. Luna almost missed the turn. The sign was low to the ground and set back from the street. She pulled into a dirt driveway and saw a small wooden plaque, hanging from an aluminium pole, with the letters MGR and an arrow burned into it, pointing to the left. She followed the sign, pulled up in front of MGR's trailer. Tula jumped out the window and rolled in the dirt. Luna checked herself in the mirror, brushed her naturally blonde, flyaway hair and adjusted the leather strap around her neck so that the coral and turquoise Zuni sun god rested in the notch of her collarbone. She debated whether she needed shoes.

She got out of the car, stretched her strong lanky legs—like a colt's her father said when she was born—and scanned the area for watching eyes. Satisfied there were none, she faced the sun, put her hands in prayer position, lifted her head, then bent her body over in a bow. Interrupted by a tinny sound, she straightened, turned, and saw a snarly-faced woman with a large plastic bag full of cans, staring at her. The woman raised her upper lip as if she might bark, but limped away with the bag dragging and clanging behind her.

Luna tapped on Darryl's screen door with the front of her cast iron goddess ring. The door had a missing hinge and when she knocked it swung toward her at a crooked angle and creaked. Darryl, in his bare feet, chewing on a toothpick, emerged from the darkness. A television hummed in the background.

"Are you Darryl?"

"Hey. Just a second." He closed the door. Luna looked down at the tattered bronco rider welcome mat and noticed a turtle the size of her foot ambling toward the door. Tula, satisfied with her dirt bath, bounded to Luna's side and sniffed at the turtle. Luna put her on leash and held her back. When Darryl returned he was wearing three-inch high snakeskin cowboy boots. "Come on in. That's Jake. He's waiting for his bath."

"I'm Luna, a friend of Bill's from Wickenburg. Can I bring my dog in?"

"Sure. Good old Bill. How's he getting along up there?"

Darryl's trailer smelled of cabbage and marijuana. "Have a seat," he said, motioning to the kitchen table. The chair seats were covered with what looked like placemats encased in yellowed plastic, made from old maps of Arizona.

Luna fingered the chair seat. "Oh, this is interesting."

"Thought of it myself."

Luna sat down and crossed her legs. Darryl looked at her ankle. "Nice bracelet."

He took a drag from a hand-rolled cigarette. "Care for a toke?"

"Oh, no thanks."

"Medicinal. You can buy it off the Internet these days. Complications from Nam, you know. Bill tell you about our time there?"

"No. I didn't know." She hoped Darryl wouldn't go into any details. She knew these guys had flashbacks, sometimes got violent. Everyone needs healing, she thought. "Bill said you might have a trailer I can rent."

Bill, an ex-biker turned short order cook, had been Luna's boyfriend back in Wickenburg, where she'd worked the breakfast and lunch shift at the Red Kettle café. Bill's Denver omelettes were a local favourite. Luna never imagined herself having to work as a waitress, but she'd left her abusive husband in the dead of a cold winter night, the same way her father had left years ago, without much money.

She wanted to save enough to take a refresher course at the local massage school and eventually get a job doing that. In the meantime, she was glad to have opportunities to use her gift. A little girl, wearing a pink-sequined baseball cap, came into the café with her parents and Luna knew the girl was bald underneath. A woman who coughed too much would sit in Luna's section and Luna could tell she was terminal. When she took their orders, she'd position herself so she could send healing energy directly into their eyes. She never knew the results. Most people just passed through. But with one or two of them she could tell right away they'd been cured.

After a while, Luna moved into Bill's one room cabin outside of town. He liked to take a pee off the back deck and said if the time ever came when he couldn't do that without being seen, he'd have to move further out. He taught Luna how to use a band saw and other power tools so she could make altars and wooden goddesses. He helped her bag a dead coyote on the road. Luna buried the animal in the back of the cabin and performed a ceremony asking the trickster coyote to help her keep a wild heart. Her husband would never have allowed such a thing.

Luna lived in Wickenburg for eight months. During that time a plastic surgeon opened an office and breast implants popped up and out of every girl and woman's blouse, tee shirt and sweater. There was bragging in the Red Kettle about not having to wear a bra ever again. There was a rumour a tanning salon, offering Botox, would open soon. Luna imagined her skin shrinking, becoming like glue. She didn't understand how women could so easily assault their bodies with knives, plastic and poison. They rolled their eyes and walked away when she talked about body integrity. "I gotta get out," she told Bill. "I need more breathing room."

The day she left town, Janie, a massage therapist friend, told her that Bill had been cooking up more than omelettes. He'd been selling $10,000 shares of a non-existent solar energy business to old ladies and body workers in Phoenix and Tucson.

At the trailer park, Darryl led Luna outside. "Yep," he said. "A place just opened up two days ago." She wondered if he was in on Bill's scam. He shuffled and kicked his snakeskin-covered feet through the dirt as they walked. Luna followed barefoot. Tula trailed behind. "There's two rows of trailers, the Yavapai section and the other, where you'll be: the Yaqui side. Named for Indians, you know."

The dry empty heat singed Luna's pale scalp. She felt more at home in the desert than she had in the muggy summers and icy winters in St. Louis where she grew up, tried to be a wife and thought she'd be a mother. Alone at thirty-five, she wondered if a child would be in her future. Darryl stopped at the end of the Yaqui section, where an old light blue trailer, "a teardrop" he called it, was parked behind a small cactus garden.

"You'll need a vap," he said.

"A what?"

"A vap cooler. I got an old one. Needs cleaning but it works. You can have it for $25."

"I'll take it and the trailer. How much?"

"For a friend of Bill's, I let it go for $300 a month."

They spent the rest of the afternoon at Darryl's place, drinking beer, eating blue lime-soaked corn chips, and watching the talk shows on the fake zebra fur couch. When Darryl switched the channel and the topless maids came on, he said, "Wow, look at that. That's really something." Whenever a hard penis came Luna's way that was a signal for her. She felt funny if she didn't do something. She usually enjoyed it. They left the TV and their clothes on. They didn't speak or kiss. She raised up her thin cotton squaw skirt with the pink and green arrowhead print and turned onto her back.

Afterwards Luna said, "Hey, Darryl, did you know that the word squaw means vagina?"

He got up, zipped his pants and said, "I'll go get that vap."

Outside her new home, Luna opened the U-Haul. Bill had arranged the boxes in neat rows according to size. At twilight the temperature dropped. Heat from the day, sucked up into black asphalt, softened the uneven edges of the driveway. Crickets began to chirp. Luna breathed in the quiet desert air as the sun slid behind a small grove of palm trees behind the Yaqui section of the Papago Trailer Park.

Edna's heart calmed to fewer episodes of wild beating. Now when they started up she'd have a few shots of bourbon and a half a Valium, which would knock her out for a few hours. She'd wake before dawn and play solitaire until the sun came up. But two weeks after the first cramps in the market, walking through the breezeway where bats sometimes hung, on her way to the front yard, carrying the long iron stick that turned on the sprinkler heads, another pain shot through Edna's pelvis. Her ankles wobbled. She had to lean into the cool beige bricks that Hank had shipped in from Pennsylvania when they built the house. She waited for the pain to subside, standing so close to the bricks she could almost smell limestone.

If the pain became more constant, Edna knew she'd have to see a doctor, but would put it off as long as possible. She didn't trust them. Hank had been a hypochondriac, something he hid from everyone except Edna. He felt it was a flaw in his character. He saw a doctor at the first sign of any discomfort. When he went to the hospital for the last time, he thought he had a stomach ulcer. He only wanted tests but ended up dying from a blood clot that mysteriously appeared in his leg.

At first Edna couldn't stand to be in the house alone. She considered selling and going back to Chicago. Her dark mahogany furniture didn't look right in Phoenix. But other people lived in her former home now and though she complained about the heat, she found she was looking forward to another sunny winter. She switched to Hank's side of the bed. It felt more spacious, closer to the bathroom and to the hallway door that led to the rest of the house. But she still couldn't sleep.

No matter what the weather or where she'd lived, the first thing Edna did in the morning was open the back door to air out the house and let the new day in. Since Phoenix nights were warm, she thought she might sleep better outside. She set up a day bed on the screened-in back porch and fell asleep listening to crickets and lonely dogs. In the mornings, she'd settle herself in a chair with a cup of spiked coffee, her legs up on an ottoman and read the paper. She taught herself to imitate the cooing of mourning doves. Groups of them would peck around near the bird of paradise bush in the backyard.

She swam every day, naked, except for the white bathing cap with rows of raised rubber in the shape of waves that protected her hair colour. Back in Chicago, Edna swam at the Beverly Country Club, a long way from the muddy swim hole with the swinging tire overhead where she first learned to swim from cornflower blue-eyed Jimmy Nesbitt, the only local farm boy she'd had any interest in. After he lost a leg in a tractor accident he refused to see her. Edna wanted to stay by his side but later she was glad he'd made that decision. She might have felt obligated. Jimmy was the first to put his mouth on her nipples while they treaded water in the swimming hole and she'd promised to let him go further next time. Then the tractor went out of control and Jimmy's father couldn't stop it before it ate up Jimmy's leg.

Beverly Country Club didn't allow blacks or Jews. Edna thought it would have been a more interesting place if they had. While Hank made business deals on the golf course, Edna, in the dressing room, slipped on a black Lycra swimsuit, like a skin, up her legs and over her naturally firm body. The crisscrossed straps lined up perfectly with the white imprint on her tanned shoulders. Hank was right; she had a very male looking back, except for her feminine scapulas, perfectly shaped wings, which Hank said could take her anywhere if they ever unfolded.

Edna looked in the mirror, adjusted the suit at her hips and ran her hands over her waist. On thin days, she fantasized about keeping pace with the young hard-muscled jocks that sometimes swam in the lanes next to her; their speedy bodies cutting though water like sleek silver bullets. On bloated days, before her period, she felt like a whale swimming through pea soup.

In the beginning of summer, when the pool opened, she walked by the baby pool noting which women were pregnant again and remembered how she'd felt; stuffed sausage arms, bloated stomach, thighs and hips spreading, aching breasts, everything engorged, horrified by how much her body changed in only two months, and told herself she was relieved she didn't have to stay the course.

Inhaling the sun, she scanned the pool for thrashers,

men who beat the water with every stroke, making so many waves only another thrasher could swim next to them. She chose an empty lane at the shallow end, stuck one "Fire Engine Red" toenail in the water, then slipped her feet in. She sat a while watching her toes shine, then lowered her body, checked her watch for a starting time, held her breath, and took the plunge. She gulped gracefully at the air, turning her slightly lifted head from side to side, sensitive to possible waves made by thrashers. Back and forth, pushing off, gliding, front, back and sidestroke, she gradually created a rhythm. After a while she was only aware of the sparkling sun flashing what she imagined as cave drawings on the bottom of the pool.

Afterwards, she sat shaded by a red and white-striped umbrella and had lunch while waiting for Hank; a rare cheeseburger, no ketchup, and a Martini with two extra olives.

Now with thinning skin, bluish from aging capillaries, Edna was grateful to have her own pool. She understood why older people went to places like Sun City to live. No apologies for showing one's age, although maybe that was different now with all the plastic surgery.

Today, Edna swam ten laps, then flipped the sides of her bathing cap up and floated on her back with her eyes closed. The pale turquoise water gently lapped around her ears.

On Sunday mornings, Edna sat at the kitchen table, spread open *The Arizona Republic* and went through it page-by page, front to back. She didn't read the paper so much as scan the highlights. One Sunday she ran across an introductory coupon for six sessions at the new Shapely Body Institute that had just opened in Scottsdale. "Let our new state of the art machines do the exercise for you," the ad said. Edna decided to give it a try.

Maybe the cramping was a sign she needed more exercise. Edna could remember when there was no such thing as "fitness." Most women were happy to do a few spot exercises for the stomach and thighs and take a walk in the evening, after dinner, with their husbands. In addition to swimming, Edna had been doing a half an hour of Jack LaLanne for years, which she started after she got married, to make sure she kept her figure. She watched Jack on black and white television everyday in her bare feet, wearing black tights and a leotard with a thick terrycloth headband over her hair in case her scalp started to sweat. Jack's wife, Elaine, and his white dog were on the show. Edna thought Jack treated the dog better than his wife, although Edna did find her slightly annoying, smiling in that demurely fake way when he corrected her form with a tone of disdain. If the dog had been able to exercise, Jack probably would have corrected him too. After Jack went off the air, Edna continued to do jumping jacks; leg lifts for inner and outer thighs, sit-ups; and while gripping tiny pink barbells, three different exercises for upper arm flab, which seemed to hang lower each year no matter what she did.

Some months ago, the Arizona Bank became the Shapely Body Institute. It looked the same except for the Mexican pots full of marigolds at the entrance. Inside, the lights were fluorescent bright and the staff of girls, too young and perky. Edna left her sunglasses on.

A young woman with pink hair and many coloured symbols tattooed on her left arm, one of which looked Masonic, approached. "I'm Crystal, your personal technician. Mrs. Harwood, you are going to look great and lose inches to boot." She took Edna to a soft pink room without mirrors and showed her the five table machines designed to pulsate specific areas of the body. She pulled a tape measure from her pocket and began to measure Edna's body parts.

"How did your parents choose your name?" Edna asked.

"From 'Dynasty.'"

"I thought so." I would never have named a child that, Edna thought.

Crystal wore black suede boots, with a flap that folded over at the top. On the backs in white block letters were written the words "Angel" on the right boot, and "Devil" on the left.

"Which are you?" Edna asked.

Crystal laughed and said, "Oh, Angel, of course. We all have both qualities in us, don't you think?"

"I guess that's true."

"Of course different people have different proportions." Crystal patted one of the exercise tables. "Jump up on this one first, Mrs. Harwood. On your tummy."

Crystal strapped her to the table with thick canvas belts that reminded her of a prisoner about to be executed.

Edna spoke through the face hole. "There was a faith

healer named Brother Billy who came to my small town every August. He'd set up a tent on one of the farms and preach every day. He healed and I think also harmed a lot of people. I don't know in what proportions."

Crystal flipped a switch and the table began to vibrate. "Only God can judge. Isn't that right, Mrs. Harwood?"

IV

Edna wasn't sure how a widow was supposed to act so she copied other women she saw in the market, alone, with their brave-boned postures, wearing fake smiles, too much rouge and eye-liner, flowered sundresses, their wrinkled cleavage and flabby arms showing, balancing themselves on high heeled strappy sandals they'd gotten too old to walk in. The sad ones tried to get sympathy by asking the bag boys for help when they didn't need it. After experimenting, wearing an appropriate amount of rouge, Edna found that one or both of these acts worked well in public depending on the situation. Sometimes she felt confused about how she wanted to be treated. Even if she wasn't in the mood for sympathy, it seemed the older she got the more younger people talked to her in a singsong patronizing tone, like she was a child or a small pet.

One day in the fruit section of the market, as Edna sniffed one lemon after another testing for sweetness, an unkempt woman came up beside her and began moving her hands through the air over the pink grapefruits. Her nails were dirty and the joints of her fingers knobby. Edna had read that that was from too much knuckle cracking. The woman wore a big silver ring with a protruding milky white stone held in place with star-shaped prongs. Edna had seen her in the market before but not this close up. Suddenly, she felt another twinge in her pelvis and dropped her bag of lemons. She tried the breathing exercise but it didn't work. Edna put her hand over her belly and said to the cramp, "Knock it off."

"Were you talking to me?" The tall wiry woman's stringy blonde hair hung over the sides of her face and her nipples showed through her flimsy top.

"No, I wasn't."

"Am I in your way? I was just checking to see which of these grapefruits wanted to go home with me." The woman told Edna she'd just moved to town and was scouting the markets to see where she best resonated with the food. "Are you okay? I noticed you were holding your stomach."

"I'm fine." Edna snapped a plastic bag off the roll above her head.

"Are you sure you don't need some help? I could at least pick out some lemons for you. I just need to touch your arm so I can feel your energy."

"No, thank you." Edna pulled her shoulders back.

"I love that you're wearing a Christmas tree in the summertime. I do that. Leave my tree up all year long."

"If you must know, it has nothing to do with Christmas. It just so happens December 25th is my birthday. This is a birthday pin."

"Ah, born on the cusp of prophecy. You're very independent." The woman pushed her hair behind her ears revealing silver and turquoise earrings in the shape of little faces.

"What?"

"But you have a tendency to be isolated and withdrawn. You don't care if people like you, which gives you a lot of freedom."

Edna had no idea what the woman was talking about. She was tired of feeling obligated to speak and exchange smiles with strangers. When she was young, men she didn't know would come right up to her on a street corner and say, "Smile, honey. It can't be all that bad." What if a loved one had just died? Why couldn't they stand to see an unsmiling woman?

Edna hadn't felt comfortable in her skin as a young woman. Other girls, like her older sister Flo, were lighthearted, with smiles that spread over their faces, for no reason, in the wink of an eye. At one point it occurred to Edna that Flo was so easy going because she didn't get any beatings. This disparity was what led Edna to believe she was illegitimate and that's why her mother picked on her. She was the only redhead in the family. She didn't have her father's angular nose and jaw. She'd heard that people sometimes hid secrets in the family Bible so she searched there but found only three one-hundred dollar bills bookmarked at the twenty-third psalm.

Now that she was older and a widow, Edna realized she could get away with things like bumping into people who were in her way or stepping on their feet and then pretending she'd lost her balance, which she decided to do with the barefooted woman in front of her.

"Oh, I'm so sorry. Did I hurt you?"

"It's okay." The woman picked up her foot and began massaging her big toe. "I understand where you're coming from."

"What? It was an accident." Edna spun her cart around and headed to Liquor for her usual half-gallon of Ancient Age. Before checking out she picked up some frozen dinners and a Sara Lee Fudge cake. Thank God two people came up behind her in line before the grapefruit woman got there.

At the age of nine, Luna cured her fourteen-year-old cat, Jupiter, formerly known as Fluffy, (Luna's mother wasn't good at naming cats or people) from a limp. It was the first sign of her healing power. Jupiter injured his leg jumping from a ten-foot high bookcase. Luna's father, who had healing powers of his own, encouraged her to try and cure him. She didn't know exactly what to do so she followed her intuition; closed her eyes, held her hand over Jupiter's leg and made sounds. After a few minutes, he rolled over and purred. Luna saw white light emanating from the fur on his paws. Three days later, Jupiter stopped limping.

Like her father, Luna loved the southwest. She was ten when he took her on one of his business trips, selling and stocking vending machines. Harry wanted to relocate to Arizona so his company gave him part of the southwest territory, which consisted of towns like Winslow, Window Rock and Four Corners.

Luna remembered him in the just-lit morning, his narrow head and body making a long shadow in their St. Louis tract-house driveway as he loaded up the trunk of the old blue Dodge with his supplies. He hung a water bag on the front of the car. "We might need this in the desert." It had a red faded flower on it with the words "*Desierta Bolsa de Agua*" centred underneath.

Every morning, on the road, after they slept at places like the Sleep Wigwam that had tepees for rooms, they'd eat breakfast at coffee shops and Luna was allowed to order pancakes with extra butter and syrup. In Holbrook, they stopped to see the twenty-eight foot dinosaur, "As tall as Bob's Big Boy" a sign said. A long tongue hung out of the dark cavern of its mouth. Every afternoon, they'd stop for lemonade and beer. Luna wanted to take a detour to see Montezuma's Castle but her father said he couldn't spare the time. At the Pow Wow Trading Post, Harry bought a beaded Indian coin purse with an Indian's feathered head tooled on one side. He slipped pennies into it before presenting it to Luna with his long card-flipping magic fingers. "A gift from the Chief," he said. "We'll come back another time to see Montezuma's Castle." They never did.

But a year after the trip with her father, Luna went on a field trip to Montezuma's Castle with her Camp Fire Girl troop. Lying awake in her sleeping bag at the Indian ruin after the others had gone to sleep she heard the low hollow sound of rattles and the voice of an ancient man who told her to look for a comet in the night sky. When she saw it shoot past the moon, she felt the fine red dust of Indian power penetrate her skin and knew she had a gift. In the morning she told Mrs. Hancock, the troop leader, and the other girls what had happened. They laughed and called her crazy. But underneath their phoney voices Luna heard chanting and rattling.

It was after what she called her initiation at Montezuma's Castle that Luna changed her name to the moon. Like Fluffy, Luna needed to be under a different vibration than the name her mother had chosen for her, which was Maureen. She never felt like a Maureen or a Mo, the nickname other kids called her. "You can't have a Mexican name," her mother said. Luna had come to love the Spanish language. Her favourite word was *maquillaje* even though, unlike other girls her age, she didn't like wearing make-up.

Luna wrapped up her Camp Fire Girl neck scarf and navy blue felt vest, heavy with honour beads, mostly brown ones representing outdoor crafts, packed them in a lingerie box, and resigned from the Camp Fire Girls. It was just as well. Mrs. Hancock had threatened to kick her out if she didn't earn some homemaker craft beads, which entailed washing and waxing a small floor, learning to iron, organizing a kitchen cupboard and practicing to become a charming hostess.

Instead, Luna began to read about goddesses. She learned all their names and the different powers they possessed. She studied astrology and numerology and practiced rituals in her bedroom. She liked looking at pictures in *National Geographic* of dark-skinned naked people with designs on their faces. Painting one's face for a spiritual purpose made sense. She earmarked the pages and kept the magazines under her bed. A gold speckled rock her father brought her from the Grand Canyon served as a paperweight. On Saturdays, she'd paint the designs on her face; leave them on all weekend, refusing bribes of money from her mother to wash them off. When her father wasn't away on business, he let her decorate his face like a native man.

Now, even though her trailer rent was cheap, Luna wondered how she would survive. She worried about supporting her dog, Tula, too. Fear about money had kept her from leaving her husband sooner than she did. She'd tried to heal him, sent white light into his heart while he slept, but her powers had the opposite effect; he became more enraged. Then came the night she knew she couldn't take his abuse anymore and, fuelled with a shot of courage, she left.

Waitressing wouldn't pay the bills. Neither would an office job. Besides, Luna couldn't picture herself sitting at a desk all day. She decided to try, for the first time, to make money with her gift.

Judging by what other people in the field charged, she could make between sixty-five and a hundred dollars an hour. She wondered if Darryl would trade some of next month's rent for a healing session. In the past, people came by word of mouth and she took donations. After she got married, her husband, in a condescending way, told her not to make too much money or she'd put him in a higher tax bracket.

Darryl agreed to help her design a flyer on his computer, to put up at the health food stores. As soon as she could afford it, she'd get a computer of her own and put an ad in the *Phoenix Whole Life Journal* with a picture of herself.

"You know there's another psychic who lives in the park, name of Kimberly," Darryl said. "Yavapai side, C-3, has a neon sign in her window that says 'Physic.' I've only seen a couple people go in there. She takes care of a bunch of turtles, gave Jake to me as a gift after I built her a ramp. She's disabled."

So he would do a trade, thought Luna. "I think I've seen her. What kind of psychic work does she do?"

"Not sure. Something about aliens and angels. She makes video tapes of them."

"That can be tricky. I'll have to introduce myself. Can you put an image of one of the tarot cards at the top?"

"Sure."

Luna didn't need the cards to do a reading but she thought she'd get more calls if she advertised the tarot.

As a teen-ager, Luna's father trained her to read minds and predict the future. On Sunday afternoons, despite her mother's pouting about being left alone, (Luna's mother didn't like to share her husband) Harry took Luna to the shopping mall where they'd sprawl their long, lean-limbed bodies on a bench near the escalator. He'd close his eyes until an image appeared from the deepest part of his spine. And when he opened his eyes they'd be darker than before, almost black. Luna saw tiny gold specks in the centres. He'd speak his predictions of people riding on the escalator; car accident in six months, dead foetus, he's about to inherit money, but it won't change his life. Luna would take a turn; her sacrum would start to ache as images came to her. With the people at the mall, they never knew if their predictions were right, but with kids from Luna's school and his friends, Harry kept track of events. He told Luna they were accurate eighty-eight percent of the time.

While Darryl worked on the flyer, Luna made a list of health food stores in the area. She wished she had the money to shop organic but she did the next best thing; searched out a regular grocery store with high vibration food. She'd checked out six of them before settling on Bayless market where she'd noticed several lonely widows, like that obstinate one she ran into the last time she was there.

Since she'd moved to Phoenix, she hadn't had opportunities to use her gift. Maybe she'd do some secret healing work at the market.

"Here," said Darryl, clicking to a page with pictures of different tarot decks. "What's your pleasure?"

Luna pointed to the Egyptian deck.

"Hey, look at this. There's a Moon card," he said.

Darryl dragged the image onto the flyer and enlarged the white-haired woman holding up the moon, as a pack of coyotes slept at her feet.

It still didn't seem like Hank was completely dead. At the market, Edna caught herself looking at anniversary cards. She'd done the same thing around the time of his birthday and on Valentine's Day. She'd glance into her cart and realize that once again she'd dropped Old Spice deodorant in without thinking.

It seemed like he was off on an extended trip bird hunting or fishing at Saguaro Lake. The first thing Hank bought after they moved to Phoenix was a boat. He named it "Second Chance" and had a house for it built behind the backyard with a huge door so he could roll it out into the alley and hook it up to his car.

Edna liked how he'd looked, dapper, sporty and slim in his all-white boating outfit. When he thought she wasn't looking he played with his Captain's hat in the mirror, pulling it down on his balding head, testing different ways to angle the brim, making an awning of shadow that turned his bright eyes the colour of navy blue. He read boating magazines and bought an elaborate compass, his first purchase on the Internet. No matter how he explained it to her, Edna couldn't understand what special things it did besides point its fancy red glowing needle in the right direction.

She missed hearing the stories about Hank's adventures with his new friends from the Masonic lodge. On one outing to the lake, Arthur, who couldn't swim, fell in the water. He weighed so much, all the guys had to jump in to save him. When he came back from a hunting trip, Hank told Edna that Tom's eyes were so bad he couldn't even hit a wounded quail on the ground. Edna didn't think that was funny, but Hank laughed loud with his mouth wide open. His whole body shook and his eyes turned red. Hank's voice made him appear taller than five-foot nine. Sometimes he seemed to tower over Edna. She always wondered what kind of father he would have been.

Sometimes Edna felt glad to be alone, her behaviour unobserved. Not that Hank was that observant but if he could see the living room furniture covered in plastic, see her wearing wrinkled clothes, drinking before noon, abandoning her large bath and dressing area for the kitchen sink where she now washed her face and brushed her teeth, he would be shocked. The days of worrying about what mood Hank would be in when he came home, were over. At the dinner table he'd suddenly shout things like, "For God's sake, Edna, where are the rolls?" She thought his outbursts were about things that had happened at work or something she'd done wrong or that she'd never gotten pregnant again. She'd been afraid to ask. She hoped after he retired things would be different. Now she would never know.

A month later, at the beauty shop, Rose told Edna about a group called Smokenders that had helped her nephew stop smoking. "Maybe this would help your cramps, *Señora.*"

Hank introduced Edna to smoking and drinking after they met in the summer of 1948 at a picnic on the bank of the Beaver river, when she was nineteen. She was wearing a thin white cotton dress. Ordinarily she would have worn a slip, but it was too hot. Hank offered her a cigarette. "You don't have to inhale." He said he liked seeing her legs through the dress and that his father owned a furniture store that would eventually be his.

After years of smoking, Edna told herself that she didn't inhale much, but she couldn't deny she had a smoker's cough. At the Smokenders meetings, she learned to keep track of every cigarette she smoked by making a mark on a little chart that fit into the plastic sleeve of her cigarette pack. She was instructed to keep all the butts in a glass jar, open it up and smell it several times a day and gargle with Lavoris after every meal to cut down on cravings after eating. Edna tried talking to a man there, twenty-five years younger. She knew because at the first meeting they had to say their ages. She found herself feeling sexual when she looked at him.

Before she lost the baby and her periods ended early, Edna had enjoyed sex with Hank. She didn't have much to compare it to except the night, after drinking too much, she lost her virginity to one of the lumbering farm boys. It should have been Jimmy. The act was over before she had time to get through the pain. At eighteen, when she travelled the ten miles to town to interview for a secretarial job, Mr. Hodson, the owner of the bookstore, invited her to lunch where she had three glasses of wine. They ended up in a hotel room and Edna had her first orgasm. Later, with Hank, she had no trouble, as did many of her married friends who said they faked it most of the time.

But after the miscarriage and more so during menopause, sex with Hank became painful and began to feel like a pressure-filled obligation that she eased with a shot of bourbon or a martini. When Hank fell asleep, she masturbated with the free toothbrushes from the dentist that in the past she'd saved for houseguests.

Now at Smokenders, Edna asked the man named Dusty, "How many did you smoke this week?" He didn't answer. He half-smiled with a hint of disgust and annoyance on his face. She didn't let that stop her. "Did anyone ever tell you, you have bedroom eyes?" At that moment, Edna wished she'd had a facelift. Dusty turned his back and avoided her after that. When she was younger, flirtatious remarks worked on men like Marv Gelson, a friend of Hank's. She'd wink at Marv from across the room; take the flirtation just to the point of danger. Hank would never let her out of his sight. Edna's mother had told her, "If you want to keep a husband like Hank, you'd better keep him guessing. He can always find someone in his own class." She'd married up, as her mother said about any girl that didn't marry a farm boy.

Edna watched her manners and dress at all times. In Hank's presence, she pretended she was used to dining in fine restaurants, wearing expensive jewellery and riding around in a Cadillac. After her engagement, Edna liked visiting the farm and showing off her new clothes, emerald bracelet and diamond rings to her mother, her sister, Flo, and the other farm girls. Edna had done okay for herself in spite of her mother.

At seventy, Edna didn't care enough about attracting another man or she might have considered getting a face-lift or at least some Botox. She'd seen advertisements for vaginal reconstruction. She couldn't imagine what that would entail.

The Smokenders meetings ended and Edna didn't smoke for two weeks. Rose suggested she get involved with people her own age. "Join the Sun City Senior Citizens Club," she said, "They have dances. Your colour is nice and fresh. You should go this week."

Edna had tried going out to eat, but in a sea of couples she felt lonelier than she did at home. Where were all the widows and widowers? She wasn't too familiar with the Beatles, but she read that when John Lennon was murdered, Yoko Ono stayed in bed for a year and ate chocolate cake. Edna liked that idea, but she'd seen a picture of skinny Yoko and knew if she tried it she'd gain weight with every bite.

All Edna really wanted was to stay home and have a few drinks, but Rose was right. She should stay involved with life. She put on her usual lipstick and sprayed her neck and wrists with the Elizabeth Taylor "Diamond" perfume that Hank had given her. She'd bought the strongest magnifying mirror she could find to put on eyeliner and mascara. She couldn't believe all the lines in her face. She didn't like looking in mirrors anymore.

Edna hated the smooth-skinned volunteers at the senior centre who pretended that getting older and not having to work was cause for some kind of celebration.

She was shocked at how many women her age had faces with skin stretched as far as California on one side and Florida on the other, tucked behind their ears.

A man with glassy eyes and garlic breath asked Edna to dance. He rubbed up against her so hard she thought her bones would break. She backed away. He came closer.

"Sorry," he said. "I didn't mean to hurt you. I got a little carried away. It's just I haven't seen anyone as pretty as you for a long time. I'm Joe. Joe Wilkes."

"Edna Harwood." She probably should have made up a name. Tom, at the Goldwater bank, had warned her about men who might take advantage. This Joe might be one of them. "Don't talk to anyone about money," Tom had said. When she'd asked him how much money she had and how long it would last, he said she wouldn't have to worry if she conserved. That didn't tell her much. "What if I live to be a hundred?" Tom just laughed. She supposed if she practiced automatic smiling (her teeth still looked good), she could be a greeter at Wal-Mart. It occurred to her now that Tom could take advantage. How would she know? Hank had left him in charge. Edna never saw a bank statement.

Joe seemed clean but his collar was frayed, his pants a little too shiny, but his shoes were polished. He still had some hair and a neat white moustache. Joe looked better than most of the other men at the dance, but he was nothing compared to Hank. Edna wondered where she could go to meet someone like her husband. She kept dancing with Joe. She did like the feeling of a man's arm around her waist and he was a good dancer. He spun her in and out of a twirl. The black and white squared linoleum made Edna dizzy and she felt a cramp coming on. She put her hand over her belly.

"Something wrong?" asked Joe.

"It's nothing."

"Are you sure?"

"I'm sure. Now it's passed."

She wondered how old he was and if he had any money.

"First time here? Haven't seen you before," he said as he led her off the dance floor to a wobbly table. The band began to play "Bye, Bye Blackbird."

"Ah, the Count," said Joe.

"Do you come here often?'

"Oh, about once a week."

"Well, I'm not really looking for anyone. You know what I mean? Do they serve liquor here?"

"You bet. How about a friend?"

"What?"

"Maybe you could use a friend."

"Maybe." Edna noticed Joe's shirt had a monogram on the pocket. Part of the stitching on the "W" was missing, but she took the monogram as a sign that at one point he'd been successful. "What business were you in?"

"I was a medical doctor back in Michigan."

"Really?"

"I lost my license because of an unfortunate turn of events, but I became the top Met Life salesman ten years in a row."

Edna thought the doctor part of his story was a tall tale.

The waitress, a coyote thin woman, about Edna's age

(see, Edna told herself, if need be I could get a job) approached wearing purple pants and a saguaro cactus vest over a black western shirt. (Edna wasn't crazy about the outfit). "What can I get you folks?"

"Hi, Annie. We'll have two pieces of that delicious chocolate cake and two bourbons, straight up," said Joe. "With a water back. That is how you like it, isn't it Edna?"

"Well, yes I do. How did you know?"

"Lucky guess. Are you a church going woman, Edna?"

Annie brought the cake and drinks to the table right away. Joe took a bite. "Nice and moist."

Edna tried to ignore the crumbs that hovered on his moustache.

"My husband was a Mason, 33rd degree. It's a secret society and they have their own religion. His loyalty was to his lodge. I had to join the Eastern Star. Those women were so competitive, bragging all the time about how great their husbands and children were. They used to tell me the only thing that would make me truly happy was to have children. Thank God I was a good bowler." Edna pushed her hair back fingering her freshly coloured waves. "The best they had on their league, so they accepted me right away. They'd send out calling cards for afternoon tea parties. What a bunch of crap. I needed a drink before I went to those parties. But I grew up Lutheran and I still say the twenty-third Psalm every night."

"The Lord is my Sheppard, I shall not want…"

"You know it."

"Sure I do. You live alone, Edna?"

"Yes, and I like it that way." She didn't want him to get any ideas.

"Children?"

"No. You?"

"Never had the inclination although now I wouldn't mind a grandchild. I'm very handy around the house. I bet you could use some help."

"Oh. So you come here looking for work?"

"A little of that. Friends. Maybe a girlfriend. You never know."

Edna had been thinking that a windbreaker by the pool would be nice in fall when the weather changed, when the winds came up and gave her a chill while she was swimming. Was he strong enough to build something like that? "Would you be averse to doing some cleaning?"

"Not at all. What kind of cleaning?"

"Big jobs like windows and floors. Things that are difficult for me to do now. And I'd like a windbreaker in the backyard. Of course I'd pay you."

"Let me give you my number." Joe pulled a grocery store coupon and a tiny pencil from his jacket pocket. As he wrote, Edna noticed his hand shook a little and his fingers were stained with nicotine. That's nasty, she thought. Maybe she could convince him to switch to filtered.

Edna only had one cramp that evening. When she went to bed she had a dream about Hank. He was outside working under the hood of her Cadillac, grease all over his hands. Hank would never have done that. When he looked at her he laughed in that big noisy way that embarrassed her in public. He twirled himself around, turned into white smoke like a genie, sucked himself into the body of the car. After Hank died, Edna wondered if he would send her messages, tell her what she was supposed to do, but he never appeared until now.

She didn't know what the dream meant but she woke up with a craving for the lemon cake she used to make for Hank on Sundays.

Two weeks later when she returned home from her weekly outing to the beauty shop, market and Shapely Body Institute, where she advised Crystal not to wear her angel/devil boots and to hide her tattoos for her upcoming job interview at the Phoenician Resort, Edna opened the back door and smelled something strange, a sweaty man smell.

She walked down the hallway to her bedroom. The dresser drawers were open; some had been pulled out, the contents emptied onto the carpet. The closet door was open; clothes had been pulled off the hangers. Edna stood still, her heart pounded. She clutched her chest. Was someone still in the house?

She tiptoed to the night table. The drawer was turned over on the floor. Hank's gun was gone. Edna raced to the front door. It was wide open and the lock had been cut. She went through every room, looked in all the closets. They'd taken some of her jewellry. She gasped and covered her mouth when she got to the living room and saw that they'd emptied Hank's urn, dumped his ashes all over the carpet. Poor Hank. Who would do this? Her whole body shook. Had she brought this on by talking to Joe? Had he found out where she lived?

Edna called the police. She sat on the narrow bench in the entryway by the front door and waited for them. She'd never actually sat on the mustard coloured Chinese silk. No one had, except the Fuller brush man who had to wait one day for his money. Edna started to cry. She held her hands together so they wouldn't shake. Hank should be here. Damn him.

She felt relieved when the police came. They were young and clean looking in their crisp uniforms. They told her there had been other robberies in the neighbourhood. Two teenage boys who lived nearby, but they hadn't been able to catch them. That made more sense than Joe being the robber. He was too old to pull this off. The police wrote down everything that was missing and suggested she get a burglar alarm.

That afternoon Mary and Doug Johnson, the Mormon neighbours, came to check on her. Doug put a chest of drawers and her heavy chair with the petit point seat against the front door. They offered to have her sleep at their house, but she decided to sleep on the porch. She doubted the burglars would come back and she wanted to avoid having to accept any more casserole dishes and Jell-O moulds; unappealing Mormon bribes for her soul.

The next morning she called a burglar alarm company and a locksmith. She had a shot of bourbon, got out the vacuum cleaner, put in a new bag and vacuumed up Hank as best she could, holding back her tears. She had to stop twice when her uterus started cramping. When she finished vacuuming she unhooked the bag and emptied it into the urn. She'd never seen the ashes before. She could see pieces of carpet threads mixed in with Hank's pulverized bones. He'd wanted them sprinkled over Honolulu but Edna had never been on an airplane. She saw a crash when she was younger and couldn't get over her fear. Now she felt guilty. She and Hank took a cruise every year to Honolulu. He loved it there. Maybe she could pay someone to sprinkle his ashes.

Edna went back to the kitchen, had another shot of bourbon, made coffee and called Joe. It had been a month since she met him at the senior centre. She hoped he'd remember her. She smoked cigarettes and watched for him from the living room window. Fifteen minutes later he pulled in the driveway in an old black car that needed painting. He helped get the bedroom in order, put the mahogany dresser drawers back in their grooved slots. He made eggs and toast.

"I hope the police catch whoever did this," said Edna.

"You poor girl. I'll take care of things."

Edna let her shoulders relax. Joe sopped up egg yolk with his toast. Her mother used to do that. Edna stopped doing it after she met Hank. Soggy yellowed toast looked disgusting.

"I'm not a girl," she said.

"You know what I mean. By the way, I made a list of the materials I need to build that windbreaker. Haven't priced anything yet. I wasn't sure you'd call."

"Before you tell me how much you're going to charge a poor old widow like me, be sure to sharpen your pencil." Hank had said that to salesmen when he bought cars and large appliances.

Joe laughed. "Sure thing, Edna. My usual rate is fifty an hour but if you give me a lot of work I'll cut it in half."

"I'll have to think about it."

They sat at the kitchen table smoking and drinking coffee while they waited for the security company to arrive. She hated those non-filtered Camels of his.

Tim, a thin fellow in a dark green uniform, from Safeco Alarm Systems, suggested connecting the alarm to all the windows. "Only thing is you wouldn't be able to open them."

"We don't want that," said Joe.

Edna glared at him. Who did he think he was?

"What about attractive wrought iron bars on the windows?" Edna asked.

"That would help," said Tim.

"I like that idea," Edna said.

"Pretty soon you'll be able to get an aluminium cover and with the press of a button your entire house can be encased. That's really maximum security."

"Well, I'll be darned," said Edna. "What will they think of next?"

Joe hunched up his shoulders and lit another cigarette. "Maybe you should get a watchdog."

Edna felt a cramp coming on. "Maybe you can find me a good deal on a gun."

Since she'd put up her flyers a week ago, Luna had only had one call; a message left by a child to please call back and could she bring a cat back from the dead.

She'd posted her flyers at the Akasha Bookshop, the Thunderbolt Bookstore and the most popular health food stores. There were so many other flyers on the bulletin boards it was difficult to make space. Luna knew most of the advertising was hype and catered to the lost and lonely. But the real healers were mixed in with the fake. These days, shamans had websites and worked with people in doctors' offices.

She saw flyers for clairvoyant training, angelic frequencies healing, group channeling with the council of twelve, a workshop to learn the great Mayan prophecy for the end of time, a flyer that asked, "Would you like to become God?" And an invitation to an earth shift ceremonial sweat lodge. Luna had tried that once and had to yell out, "all my relations," which she'd been instructed to do by the medicine man, in case of claustrophobia, so he would open the flaps of the tent and let her out. People were squished together, like hot sweaty fish. She'd never experienced such profound darkness, an endless black void, which some people found calming. Luna had to have a spot of light somewhere.

She hoped people would call soon. She could feel an implosion coming on. It happened when there were no recipients for her healing energy. Without direction or focus she began to have bouts of nausea and migraine headaches. She knew she'd gone overboard, scaring that old lady in the market with too much talk about astrology and grapefruit vibrations.

She took to watching Bishop TD Jakes, a preacher from Dallas, on TV. His hopeful message about loneliness, Jesus was lonely too, possessing healing gifts, feeling misunderstood and naming the Devil as the source of distress gave Luna a temporary reprieve. TD was a former drug addict and had the charisma of a wounded healer.

The last time Luna felt afflicted with an implosion was when she lived in Wickenburg. Back then, working secretly with customers in the café and walking in the open desert by stars and moonlight provided some relief from her anxiety. But there were too many bright lights in Phoenix that ruined the night sky.

Sometimes sex was an outlet but she'd grown tired of Darryl and his habit of turning on the TV, after their time together on the couch, clicking the remote until he found those topless maids he liked so much.

Luna needed to do something to offset her implosion. If she let it take hold, she could become vulnerable to all manner of vibrational forces.

She sat in the pale yellow kitchen she'd painted over the weekend, gazing at a painting of a woman letting go of a trapeze bar, falling in mid-air, reaching for a pair of outstretched hands waiting to catch her. The painting was a gift from Deborah, an artist Luna had healed from cancer. She wished she had clients now who needed that level of help. She took a swallow of a new grain beverage she'd bought that promised to taste just like coffee. None of them ever lived up to that and this one didn't either. She got up and made herself a cup of Fair Trade Sumatra. If she was going to implode, she might as well drink real coffee. From the kitchen window she saw the sneering woman Darryl had said was a disabled psychic. She looked like she was in a permanent state of implosion, collecting cans in a giant trash bag at the neighbour's back door.

On the first day of the month, for the last two months, Luna saw Darryl, at four in the morning, walking back to his place from the Yavapai section of the park. She was sure he'd spent the night with this woman in exchange for rent, probably not the full amount. She considered bringing this up as an option for herself, but she didn't want to have sex with him anymore and asking for retroactive sex credits seemed too desperate.

Luna gulped down her coffee and went outside to help the woman.

"Hi. I'm Luna. Can I help you with that bag?"

"Why?"

"Just want to help. What's your name?"

"Kimberly. Why would you want to help me?"

"We're neighbour's. Darryl said you did psychic work and I'm a healer. We have something in common."

"Well, okay."

Luna put the last of the cans into the trash bag.

"You can drag it. It's reinforced."

"Oh. That's smart."

Kimberly led Luna down the dirt lane to another trailer to collect cans. Luna walked as slowly as Kimberly out of respect for her limitation, all the while scanning her body to see where she needed healing. Luna felt encouraged with the possibility of doing some work.

"I could use a glass of water."

"Oh?" said Kimberly.

At trailer number C-3 Luna followed Kimberly up a ramp and into a dark room with too much furniture. A large drawing of three nude women took up one of two walls.

"Oh, I love this, the earth colours and how the women lean into each other."

"I had more like that but I destroyed them. This one's my favourite. My sister painted it in Mexico. There's no place to sit. You can just move those tapes and the cat, that's Blossom, off that chair and pile them on the table."

"What are all these tapes?"

"My work. Angel aliens in action. I'll get your water." Kimberly limped to the kitchen. Her hips grazed the edges of the furniture.

Luna spotted a table next to an old cat clawed sofa filled with photographs. Some turned down. One looked like a professional photograph of Kimberly as a teenager.

"Is that you?"

"Yeah. I was 14, modelling that haircut. People told me I could have been famous. They'd be shocked to see me now." She let out a laugh that sounded more like a dog coughing. "I'll probably die on disability in this crappy trailer."

"You look gorgeous."

"I know."

"Why did you destroy your sister's art?"

"I didn't want any reminders of her. When our mother died she was in charge of everything. I didn't like that. It shouldn't have been that way. She got my mother's condo."

"Didn't you get anything?"

"Not what I deserved. I tried to sue her."

As she talked, Kimberly's body became more rigid and her speech started to slur. Luna saw her skin tighten around her bones. Kimberly's mouth contorted and both sides of her upper lip went into a snarl so all her teeth showed. Blossom let out a hiss and ran to the bedroom.

"I love my sister to death but her actions are unforgivable."

Luna didn't understand what the sister had actually done and she didn't want to escalate Kimberly's anger by asking more questions. "How do you do psychic work when your energy is so...?"

"I'm fine when I do my work. I put one of my turtles on my heart area first and that clears my energy." Kimberly went to a box of turtles on top of the TV and picked one up. "Here, put him on your chest. His name is Jessie."

"What a great feeling," said Luna holding him over her heart. "What kind of work do you do?"

Kimberly pulled a tape out of the pile and put it into an old dusty VCR. "Wait til you see. This is the most powerful one."

The tape showed a German shepherd named Laura lying in a patch of sunlight. "See the light around her body? That was right before she died. They're helping her pass over." Kimberly pointed out shadows, shapes and spots of light that she said were moving with the energy of the aliens. Luna couldn't see what she was talking about.

"The aliens are in charge, doing things on the planet and I can read their messages. They're the ones who told me my sister was no good. And I had a long talk with my mother after she died. Right now, they're showing me a picture of you as a dark skinned woman with black lace over your hair. Does that mean anything to you?"

"Well, I've been told I had a past life in Spain."

"Wow! See, I told you."

"Mind if I do some healing work on your wrist?"

"I'm afraid your energy might interfere with what my angel aliens are doing for me. I had a stroke when I was twenty-one."

"How about a little massage?"

"I guess that couldn't hurt, but it probably won't do any good."

"Sit here in front of me. Close your eyes and breathe."

Luna put her hands on Kimberly's wrist. Her tissue was ice cold and as hard as a tree trunk. Luna wanted to pull away but she began gently massaging, transferring the heat from her hands into Kimberly's wrist.

After a few minutes her wrist started to bend back and forth. She saw it moving and pulled her arm away. "Oh, my God. It hasn't done that since before the stroke. Oh. Wow. Oh. Wow." She stood up and started pacing around the trailer, bumping into the furniture. "You have to leave now. I need to be alone."

"Are you okay?"

"Fine."

"All right. I'll come by later and see how you're doing."

Kimberly contorted herself back to her usual body shape; right wrist and leg locked, sparks of anger spewed around the room. She opened the front door. "Why don't you take your healing to B-5? Fibromyalgia might give you a thrill."

Luna stepped outside and a wind came up. She covered her eyes and walked back to her trailer through the dusty air.

The following week, she knocked on Kimberly's door three different times. Luna saw her moving around inside. Her bag of cans was on the front porch, but no one answered. What good was her gift if no one wanted it?

There was nothing left for Luna to do but go roaming, as her father had taught her years ago. When Harry hit a snag with his vending machine design, felt an implosion coming on, he'd take Luna roaming with him in the old blue Dodge. He let intuition guide their direction. In the car, they played games; did mind reading and made predictions about people in other cars. If they both picked up a healing was needed, Harry would speed up and as he passed the car Luna would channel her energy into it.

Harry drove around back alleys. When he felt drawn to a house, they'd get out. Harry would lift Luna onto his shoulder to look over the fence and give him a detailed description of what she saw: the landscaping, the backyard, what kind of flowers and plants were growing, did she see any people, were there wind chimes, patio furniture, a pool? He'd mind read the life of the house, and make his predictions. Sometimes, Luna would send a healing over the fence. At one place, Luna got a picture in her mind of guns and when she looked over the fence, saw blacked-out windows. Harry carried her to the car and drove away fast, leaving a cloud of dirt in the alley.

Harry was sure his vending machine design, called Hocus Jokus, would revolutionize the business. One could buy various deception card decks, trick safety pins and other magic trinkets. Some of the slots held little booklets that revealed the secrets of levitation, instructions on how to juggle knives, how to perform the milk glass trick and push a cigarette through a card without leaving a hole. Luna designed a paper labyrinth for Hocus Jokus. She knew the Native Americans had invented the pattern but she thought they might have forgotten.

After years of work, no one wanted to buy his invention. "Cowards," he said, "too timid to take a risk." He thought magic would appeal to people who lived in the Arizona desert. He spent years installing, repairing and stocking vending machines filled with cans of soda and crappy snacks that fogged people's brains and made them fat. People needed something to feed their imaginations. Harry was ahead of his time with that kind of thinking.

Luna was sixteen when he disappeared. She tried to tune into Harry's mind. She chanted and danced her "Ladyhawk" dance to invoke the spirit of the sharp-eyed hawk to sweep the skies, find her father and deliver her message to come home or at least stay alive. She did this every day for a year in the middle of the labyrinth she'd built from stones and candles in the backyard. Luna often wondered if Harry had died somewhere in the middle of Indian Country.

Now, Luna got in her car with Tula. She closed her eyes and got the message to go north. She ended up in a wealthy neighbourhood at the bottom of Camelback Mountain called Judson Estates. There was a guard at the entrance but she saw how to get in behind the gardener's shed. She was tall enough now, taller than her father, to see clearly across most fences. Sometimes she had to jump up to get a good view but she had inherited a lanky athleticism from her father and at thirty-five, with gangly limbs and flexible joints, she moved like a twelve-year-old and could jump straight up in the air like a dancer.

The two houses Luna felt drawn to had barbed wire and cameras on top of twelve-foot high brick walls. From both, she picked up distress around marriage and alcohol. With no visual information, she channelled her awareness to clear the negative energy fields. These excursions helped keep her healing gift strong and clear.

Back in the car, she continued driving north to Bayless Market not so much on intuition but for practical reasons. She needed fruit (she'd been craving persimmons), a head of lettuce and apple juice.

At the checkout counter Luna came up behind the older woman she'd talked to before. "Oh, hi. I saw you here a few weeks ago, in grapefruits. Remember?"

The first time Edna's gardener, Fermin, met Joe; he was picking scallions and radishes in the backyard. Joe was carrying in supplies for the windbreaker. Fermin reached for his foot-long gardening shears and stood up. Joe said hello, but Fermin didn't answer, just stood there opening and closing the shears with his gloved hand until Edna came out and introduced them. After that, Fermin ignored him.

Edna felt safer with Joe around. He said it might take a year to finish the windbreaker. Edna thought he took too many cigarette breaks, but he was over seventy, out there in the heat, sweating in that raggy under-shirt. At first, he came to the house once a week, then almost every day. He took out the trash and cleaned the windows or floors. Then he and Edna spent time chat-ting, drinking bourbon and playing double solitaire.

They went to the market and rented a shampoo machine so he could clean the carpet. Edna knew the checkers and bag boys probably thought he was her boyfriend. Some of them remembered Hank. She tried to be particularly bossy in front of them so they would know he was working for her. "Put the machine in the trunk and don't bang the car." He wasn't the calibre of Hank and she felt embarrassed by his frayed around the edges appearance.

Edna told Rose, "He's no *Señor* Hank."

"But *Señora* Harwood, *es major de nada, no?*"

When the spotting started, Edna made an appointment with Dr. Mann. She'd seen him once before for a routine pap smear. His office building had a flat roof sprinkled with pink and white stones. Saguaro and barrel cactus grew in the courtyard.

Edna endured smiling nurses wearing latex gloves, their hands frozen-looking as they dragged sticky rubber-tipped wands over her pelvis. She held her breath for the gynaecological exam.

"So, how long before I kick the bucket?" she asked Dr. Mann. "I'm no spring chicken."

He laughed. "If we get that baby carriage out of there, you just might live forever."

Edna guessed he was about forty. He wore a green tie embroidered with ducks. Pictures of two blonde spanking white children at various ages adorned his consultation room along with books and magazines on duck hunting. How could anyone kill a duck? she thought. She'd asked Hank that once. "For God's sake, Edna," he'd said. "It's just a bird."

"Baby carriage?"

"The uterus. After a certain age, it's just a cancer breeder." Dr. Mann leaned back in his leather chair.

"Do I have cancer?"

"Tumours. We think they're benign but you need a hysterectomy."

"I've never been cut open in my life," said Edna,

recoiling. "My husband died in surgery. Can't I take a pill or something?"

Dr. Mann chuckled. "That won't do it. We need to get in there." From his desk drawer he pulled out a plastic model of a woman's lower body. He snapped the plastic torso in half with his thick fingers and pointed with a pencil. "Now," he said, "If we just cut here…"

Edna buttoned her sweater. She crossed her arms over her breasts.

"These tumours are very common in women who haven't had children."

"That miscarriage wasn't my fault," said Edna. "The doctor said so. I just never got pregnant again. I went through an early menopause."

"I have a theory. Sometimes these tumours are a woman's attempt to grow the baby she never had."

"That's the craziest thing I ever heard. What if I don't have the surgery? What will happen?"

"It could get worse. Most women say it's the best thing they ever did. We can leave the ovaries if you like."

"I'll have to think about it."

Dr. Mann frowned. "It's a preventative measure for someone your age. You shouldn't wait too long."

In the car Edna thought about her early menopause. No more periods and no more eggs at the age of forty-two. She suffered with migraine headaches and debilitating hot flashes that forced her to sit down or hold onto something. For relief, she drank more than usual and sometimes feared she might drink herself to death.

Sex became painful. She tried all kinds of lubricants

and hormones that made her brain foggy. At night, she'd sweat through her nightgown, sheets, pillows and mattress pad. She'd wake up soaking wet; feeling like her body was burning something out of itself. She saw the miscarried baby girl, who they'd named Emma, hovering at the end of her bed. Hank had insisted on picking a boy's name too. They decided on Howard, but Edna knew it was a girl because she'd had dreams of walking with her in a park. She looked just like Hank.

Edna would strip off her nightgown, walk naked to the living room, lie on the red silk couch and sob, knowing she was leaving permanent stains on the fabric. Her body couldn't stop crying. She muffled her tears so Hank wouldn't wake. She kept feeling she'd done something to kill the baby, but didn't know what. When Hank left for work in the morning she could cry all she wanted, even howl. She made sounds that scared her, sounds she'd never heard except Sundays when Hank watched "Wild Kingdom" on television. She'd be in the kitchen cooking a roast and she'd hear a lion roar or other animals growling or screeching. All she wanted was to be alone and mourn the loss of her baby and her eggs.

Hank came home early one day and caught her crying on the den floor wrapped in her favourite lavender-coloured satin quilt with crumpled pink tissues scattered around her head like a garland. At first she didn't know he was there. He didn't say a word, just cleared his throat. She knew that was a sign for her to get it together. He went to the kitchen and made a Martini, asked her if she wanted one. "I think I'm in menopause," she said from the floor.

"For God's sake, Edna. Use your head. You're too

young for that."

That night he just stared out the window at the two birdhouses he'd built last summer as snow collected on their mahogany-stained slanted roofs, making them as high as a many-layered wedding cake. Later that night, the electricity went out and Edna made steak sandwiches for dinner, in the dark.

Edna had missed her usual hair appointment with Rose to see Dr. Mann, but she still had to go to the market before she went home. Preoccupied with thoughts of being cut open, she put strange things in her cart; a bottle of scotch instead of bourbon, citrus scented soap with little pieces of oatmeal encased in it, instead of her white Ivory. She hadn't seen the insides of a kiwi or a pomegranate for a long time so she dropped one of each in her cart, not to eat, but to halve when she got home.

By the time Edna made it to the checkout line her groceries looked like someone else's. She unclasped her purse, pulled out her wallet and began counting money. A cart came up behind her and grazed her hip.

Oh, no. It was that strange woman. She wore a big smile as if they'd become lifelong friends after one encounter in fruit. At least this time she wasn't barefoot. Edna kept counting.

"It must mean something that I keep running into you. I use that soap. It's great for your skin."

Edna turned her back and inched her cart forward. Why wasn't this line moving? Probably some widow up there with a pile of coupons.

"That pomegranate you have there doesn't have the

best vibration. I could pick out a better one for you."

Edna didn't answer. The woman reminded her of her sister, Flo, who never knew when to back off. She'd talk you to death; go on and on, until you agreed to give her what she wanted. But what did this woman want?

Luna began rustling through her bag, pulled out a small object made of white and brown feathers, strips of leather, tiny coloured stones and other indistinguishable materials. "I don't mean to bother you, but I'd like to give you something. I think it will help."

"No, thank you," Edna said with her back turned.

The woman reached around and put the object in Edna's view. "It's dusty but it works."

Edna remembered that big silver ring from before. "What the hell is that? Are those feathers from a bird?"

"That and some fur from a special cat. It's a talisman."

"I don't care what it is, I don't want it." Edna imagined a ritual out in the woods with people skinning cats and putting them to death in the name of Satan or who knows who.

"I'm sorry," Luna said.

When Edna got home she found the feathered object at the bottom of her purse. She covered her hand with a rubber glove, pulled it out, and threw it away.

Joe was working on the windbreaker. What a day. First the doctor, then that woman. Edna poured herself a shot, drank it down and grimaced. She'd mistakenly bought Glenlivet Scotch. She didn't care if it had aged fifteen years. It tasted like the bottom of a barrel. She started a new grocery list and wrote "Ancient Age" at the top, in capital letters. She'd go back to the store tomorrow. If it weren't for Joe out there she'd take a swim in the nude. Edna put on her suit and went to the pool. She ignored Joe. She floated on her back, closed her eyes and tried to empty her mind of everything Dr. Mann had said. She heard the flat pounding of Joe's hammer, softened by the water lapping around her ears. I'll get a second opinion, she thought.

The hammering stopped. Suddenly a wave washed over her and water went up her nose. She swam toward the shallow end until her feet touched the bottom. Joe had stripped down to his boxer shorts and jumped in. He dog paddled to the four-foot mark where Edna was standing with only her head above water. Joe came closer and tried to kiss her.

She pushed on his chest. "What do you think you're doing?"

"I got so hot. In more ways than one." He grinned. His teeth looked smaller up close.

"You scared me." Edna moved to the side of the pool, put her hand on the flagstone ledge. Joe moved with her, planted himself in front of her and touched her right breast. Edna didn't move. She closed her eyes. He pulled down the top of her bathing suit. Her breasts floated, released from spandex.

"Nice," he said. He held them, went underwater and kissed each nipple. His wet moustache felt like heavy gauze.

Then he ruined everything by grabbing her hand and shoving it inside his boxers.

"How about it, Edna?"

"You have a lot of nerve." She yanked her hand out

of his pants.

"I got myself some Viagra, at a good price. We could give it a try."

"Stop this right now." She dragged her legs through heavy water to the pool steps, got out and turned to him. "I have to have a hysterectomy." She started to cry and ran into the house.

"Sorry," Joe called out. "Sorry. I didn't know."

That night, to ease cramping, Edna drank two highballs of scotch with Coca-Cola to mask the taste. She didn't normally mix drinks because it caused hangovers. She ran a bath. Lying in the tub, she thought about how Hank had never come into the pool for a kiss. He liked to be in a boat on top of the water, not in it. And he'd insisted on always being on top of her, even though she wanted to try something different. One summer night in Chicago, Edna went out to the backyard, naked, laid down on a lounge chair and moon bathed, waited for Hank to find her. It took him forever.

She'd read that a Viagra hard-on could last a long time. She wasn't sure she could take all that. She'd have to use lubricants. A part of her hoped she hadn't discouraged Joe completely. She thought of how he kissed her nipples. She slid her finger inside herself, moving in and out until she felt a release.

Dr. Mann came back to mind. Edna probed her pelvis with her fingers, trying to feel the tumours. She thought she'd wanted children but maybe she'd lied to herself and that's why she'd miscarried, never gotten pregnant again and had early menopause. Now the tumours were paying her back. She overheard a woman at the beauty shop say that not having children was the biggest tragedy of a woman's life. They all bragged about their adult children taking them to doctor's appointments and to brunch on Sundays. Edna tried to imagine Emma taking her to an expensive restaurant on Mother's Day, pulling out her chair, helping her off with her coat. The muscles around her eyes softened. She let her body sink deeper into the warm water, resting the bones of her neck on the tub pillow.

In case she became incapacitated after uterine surgery, if she went through with it, Edna decided to visit the Sunnyslope Palms nursing and assisted living home, unannounced, so they couldn't fool her with a good impression. She'd heard it was the best in Phoenix, although some years back one of the patients, a woman from Yuma, died trying to burn the place down. She wandered from her room to the Activities Centre at three in the morning and succeeded in burning up most of that building and herself. Rumours ran the gamut: the woman was crazy or she'd been treated so badly she wanted to die.

But Rose told Edna that Mildred, one of the regulars at the beauty shop, had gone to Sunnyslope Palms for rehabilitation after a hospital stay. She told Rose it was like a country club. She loved the food, didn't want to go home. Edna could believe that. Mildred wanted people to do her bidding, always asked Rose for help getting to the chair, demanded a pillow to sit on while under the dryer, complained her daughter didn't spend enough time with her. She looked sturdy enough. Mildred faked debilitation. Edna hoped she didn't get to the point where manipulating others for help was the only fun to be had.

Edna wasn't used to driving any further than Rose's and the corner market. When he was alive, Hank had done the longer distance driving. After she passed the Turf Paradise racetrack, she knew she'd gone too far. She thought of the time Hank had taken her there to bet on the horses. She'd worn a tightly woven straw hat from Brazil with a red scarf tied around the brim. What happened to that hat? They drank Martinis inside the glass-enclosed box that towered above the track. Hank brought special high-powered binoculars, his last purchase on the Internet. He was going to teach her how to use the computer. Now, it sat in the den staring at her from the desk that held the bowling trophies she'd won back in Chicago.

That day at the racetrack, after Hank showed her how to place a bet, Edna put money on a horse named Mystic Runner, a long shot. Hank thought she was crazy but she won $200. She won another $100 with January's Hope who came in second in the fifth race. Hank didn't win anything that day, but Edna had to hear how well he'd done when he'd come to the track with his Mason buddies the week before. Later, she heard him on the phone bragging about her winnings, chuckling in that condescending "can you imagine such a fluke" kind of way.

Edna finally found Sunnyslope Palms. From the street,

all she could see was a two-story sand coloured stucco building with a badly painted mural of the Phoenix Mountains. In the centre of a circular driveway, lanky-trunked palm trees and twenty-foot high ocotillo bushes bloomed with red flowers. The ends of their whip-like branches touched each other as they waved in the breeze. Behind this building were others with arched doorways, painted in various shades of beige and pink and named for the different levels of care that might be needed, depending on what disastrous event had occurred; skilled nursing, assisted living, long term care or hospice.

Edna went through a door marked "Admissions." A small grey quail had been painted in front of the "A." It was like walking into someone's living room. She rubbed her fingers over the leaves and petals of the plants and flowers. Some were real, some weren't.

The dining room was like a restaurant with tables set for four. Desert scene watercolours hung on rose coloured walls. Tables were filled with drugged up old people, eyes blank, and mouths hanging open, some without teeth. No heads turned to look at Edna. Who would she talk to? Bodies could only hold together for so long. Then they randomly came apart. Edna knew hers was next.

"I didn't expect everyone to be so old. All the women have white hair," Edna said to the director, Gwen, a British woman whose cheeriness was hard to bear. She stood so close Edna could smell her breath. Gwen didn't blink her wide eyes or let go of her smile for a moment. Edna wondered if Gwen was naturally this way or if her demeanour came from some kind of corporate training.

These days everyone who worked anywhere acted like they'd been trained by robots.

"We do have a beauty salon on the premises if you want to have your hair coloured. You have such a pretty shade of red. Is it "Red Blaze" by chance?"

"No."

"Of course a visit to the salon would cost extra."

"Well, I'm not planning to need a place like this. I have a friend who might be interested."

"I see," said Gwen. She tossed her hair back and led Edna to the physical therapy room to meet the two young men who rehabilitated "the guests" as Gwen called them. There were smiles all around. Edna remembered when her teeth were as blinding white as these boys'. She'd had the whitest teeth of any girl or boy in New Castle.

"How do you lift someone who can't walk?" asked Edna.

"No problem." The men showed her a leather contraption, like a cinch on a saddle.

"Where's the swimming pool?"

"We had to cover it over. Poor Mr. Rhodes almost drowned one night, sleepwalking. Our first priority is safety. It used to be over there where the gift shop is now." Gwen pointed out the window at a small building surrounded by Paloverde trees.

"I have a pool," Edna said.

"Once a week those that are able climb aboard our shuttle and we all go down the road to the YMCA to swim, do our exercises in the water and sit in the Jacuzzi." Gwen clapped her hands together. "We have a wonderful time. On the drive over and back we sing songs."

It had to be corporate training, thought Edna. She'd gone to a Y once, tried sitting in the whirlpool, but there were too many old men with loud voices telling war stories over the sound of swirling water. "I like to float, alone."

"Well maybe it would be fun to join in and do something different."

"I don't think so. If other people are swimming there are too many waves and the water goes up my nose."

"I'm sure we could arrange something to suit you."

"Like I said, it's not for me."

"Of course."

Edna saw a tiny piece of green food in between Gwen's bottom front teeth that she hadn't noticed before.

At the end of the tour, Gwen gave Edna the menu for the week and a list of activities offered for the day. Edna had never heard of cheese soup. Three-bean salad sounded very gassy, especially for old people. Entrees included pot roast, devilled pork chops, fish burgers on a bun, and tapioca pudding, pumpkin cake and cherry pie for dessert. Mildred must have been eating poorly at home if she thought the food here was good. The activities included Crocheting Club with Harold, Bible Study, Stretch and Fit, Flower Arranging Club, and Afternoon Social with Entertainment by Roy. He was probably an ex-lounge singer who sang off key, thought Edna. The movie "A Walk to Remember" would be shown at 5:15 in the front lobby.

"What about cards? I was an expert Bridge player back in Chicago."

Gwen's mouth opened wider. "Well, now. There's an

idea. That's something you could organize."

At home, Edna lay down on the couch in the den, rested her hand on her pelvis. What if she had to go to a place like that? Who would visit her? Until now, Edna hadn't thought about growing old and someday needing someone to take care of her. She and Hank should have adopted or considered fertility treatments. Edna wished she had a family. Only her sister, Flo, whom Edna never understood, and her two boys were left. She hadn't heard from them in years.

Edna remembered her friend Wanda who had to stay in the hospital for two weeks. She had no family; no children and her husband had died. Before Edna and Hank moved away, Edna visited her every day. The doctors couldn't find what was wrong. They gave her all kinds of tests. Some so painful they had to drug her up beforehand. She watched her friend cry in pain when the nurses touched her. Wanda kept saying, "get me out of here." Edna considered hiring a man to lift Wanda out of bed into a wheelchair and sneak her out, but where would she have taken her? Wanda finally went to a nursing home where she lived now.

Edna wondered what Emma would have done if she'd lived to see her mother grow old. "Honey?" Edna whispered. With watery eyes she remembered how Hank would cry when he listened to his Edith Piaf records. She turned toward the wall, gazed up at Hank's favourite painting, on black velvet, of a Hawaiian woman dancing in a grass skirt. They'd bought the painting in Honolulu from the famous black velvet artist, Edgar

Leeteg, who called himself the "American Gauguin." He'd originally painted the woman bare-breasted but Edna insisted, before she let Hank buy it, that Leeteg paint a strapless top on the woman. She didn't want to have to explain anything to her friends back in Chicago, or face the disapproval of the Eastern Star. For five years in a row, Edna and Hank escaped the Chicago winters for the sensual warmth of Hawaii. While there, Edna wore sweet smelling flowers in her hair and skimpy halter-tops. She bought rhinestone-studded skirts. Hank became more attentive, touching her hair, kissing her shoulders, her collarbones and earlobes. Now, Edna closed her eyes and waited for sleep. She imagined Hank kissing her wet cheeks on the deck of a cruise ship headed for Honolulu.

The next day Edna began to think about how she could get her hands on some drugs. She wanted to have the option of killing herself if the time came that she would be sick and alone. Maybe one of Rose's relatives in Mexico could get pills. She had to be careful, though. If Rose thought she was crazy she might report her and then she'd be locked up. She knew what Rose would say, "*Señora* Harwood. I am shocked. It is up to God to decide these things." And Joe couldn't help in this area.

The falling out feeling grew worse. The pain made Edna's legs weak. She had to lie down in the dewy grass of her backyard one morning as she snipped flowers from the yellow rose bush. Poor Joe had been working so hard he had to take a day off. After the kissing incident, he'd hit his hand with the hammer. He said his whole body ached. The doves cooed and Edna cooed back. She'd gotten so good at making their sound she thought they saw her as one of them. Now, as she lay in the grass, they came close and nudged gently, tickling, caressing her bare ankles with their tiny soft-feathered heads. Edna thought maybe she was dying and they wanted her to fly with them. The sun struck out and appeared over the boathouse roof. A whole house for a boat. What a crazy thing, she thought. Waves of orange heat penetrated Edna's body as she fell asleep in the grass, the crown of the magnolia tree spread over her like a shield.

Edna awoke to someone's voice.

"You-hoo. Are you hurt?"

Edna squinted into the sun and saw a blonde-haired woman on the ledge of the wall by the boathouse, perched on her hands and feet like a spider with giant hairless limbs ready to crawl down the bricks.

"I'm coming over," she said. The woman jumped into the yard and came toward Edna. She wore a white western skirt and a tank top trimmed with tiny silver bells. Strands of seashells, circling her left wrist and arm and ending just below her elbow, rattled when she walked. She looked familiar.

"Who are you?"

"I'm Luna. I was walking back there and I picked up your vibration."

"What?"

"I sensed there was a sister in trouble on the other side of those bricks. Can you get up?"

"I don't know. I fell asleep." Edna rolled over and tried to push herself up. "My legs are too weak. Do I know you?"

"From the market."

Oh, no, thought Edna.

Luna knelt beside her. "What's your name?"

"What do you think you're doing climbing over my wall? This is private property."

Luna closed her eyes and began to circle her hands in the air over Edna's pelvis. She made low mumbling noises. Seashells softly jangled.

"What are you doing?"

"Wow. What's going on here? I feel a lot of heat."

"That's because it's hot out here."

"This may seem strange to you but I'd like to send some sound into this area."

"What?" Edna felt trapped in the yard with this woman. What if she went in the house? She could steal me blind.

Luna began chanting, softly at first and then she made deep guttural noises, like growling, sounds Edna remembered making during menopause. Her muscles tensed. "You'd better stop that." She hoped the Mormon neighbour's couldn't hear. They'd have a field day with this. Edna used to close the windows when Hank got too loud.

After a few minutes Luna stood and said, "Let's see if you can get up now."

The afternoon sun hung heavy on the leaves of the magnolia tree. Edna's whole body began to perspire.

She felt something penetrate her thin limbs, covered in her new no-iron slacks and blouse, like a pale light that helped lift her through gravity. She rose up, balancing herself against Luna's body.

"Well, I'll be darned, I'm standing."

"A doctor told me once I was better than ultrasound."

Whatever that means, thought Edna. Her legs wobbled. "Were you saying someone's name?"

"Bau-Gula and Sophia, the black Madonna. The Goddesses of Healing and Body Wisdom."

Edna didn't want to ask who they were. "Well, thank you for your help."

They stood in the shade of the magnolia tree.

"You should be able to walk now. I never did get your name."

"Edna." She took a few steps. "I think I'm better."

"Is there someone you can call to check on you?"

"Not really, but I'll be fine."

"Do you have Life Alert?"

"Oh, I don't need anything like that."

"Are you sure there's no one you can call?" A piece of magnolia blossom fell at Edna's feet.

"Well, there's Joe. He does work around here, but when I ask him for help he tries to take over and I don't like that."

"Let's go inside and I'll give you my phone number."

"That's nice of you but really not necessary." Edna thought maybe Luna wanted to get inside to "case the joint."

Luna pulled out a pencil and piece of paper from the grey suede bag she wore around her neck and wrote down her number. "Couldn't hurt to have it. I'll check on you next week."

"No. I'll be fine."

"Just please take my number." Luna put it in Edna's hand, then walked across the yard. Before scaling the wall, she turned and said, "I'll be back next Friday."

"No, really..."

That night, Edna felt another cramp. She remembered Dr. Mann's diagnosis and all she'd seen at the nursing home.

Maybe this Luna knew where to get some drugs.

The following week, Luna rang Edna's doorbell at six in the morning. She carried a rectangular straw bag containing drawing pads, crayons, silver bells and bunches of sage and dried herbs. The bottom of her skirt rustled in a momentary breeze. The air, still hot for most of the day, had begun to crisp up in the early morning. An almost imperceptible orange blossom smell hinted that fall was on the way.

Putting a terry cloth robe over her cotton sleep bra and wrinkled gardening shorts, Edna left her game of solitaire on the kitchen table and thinking it was the paperboy collecting money, answered the door. "Oh, it's you. You didn't need to come back. I'm fine." For the past week, Edna's cramps and spotting had lessened. She hadn't craved as many afternoon shots of bourbon. She drank her usual five anyway, out of habit, but she didn't need them.

Luna scanned Edna's energy body with her hands. Yes! she thought. I'm back on track.

"What are you doing?"

"I'm glad you're better, but we still have work to do. Can I come in?"

"Well, I guess." Edna was leery of what strange thing Luna would do next but she didn't know how to get rid of her and whatever she'd done in the yard last week had helped.

"Put on some water, Edna, and we'll have a cup of special tea. Do you have a teapot?"

Edna led her to the kitchen, filled the kettle and turned on the stove. She opened a cupboard and pointed to a hand painted Limoges teapot on the top shelf. "You're so tall, you get it down." She decided to go along with Luna. What harm could there be in having tea? It was more interesting than playing solitaire.

The three inches of bangle bracelets Luna wore made a deep jingling sound, like a wind chime in a breeze, as she stood on her tiptoes and reached for the pot. "This is pretty," she said.

At the table, Edna broke up her solitaire game, pushing the cards into a pile. "I wasn't going to win that one anyway."

"I'll do a reading for you sometime."

Edna didn't want a reading. All there was to know about her future was how bad it would get before she died.

Luna sat down, took a small wicker basket from her bag, set it on top of the teapot, pulled some dark green leaves and yellow flowers from one of the bundles and crushed them slightly in the palm of her hand, "to release the oils," she said. She put the herb in the basket, poured hot water over it and dunked up and down.

"Is that going to leave stains? I've hardly used that pot."

"Don't worry." Luna poured the tea into the pear and strawberry painted cups. "This is Chaparral."

"Doesn't that grow in the desert? Is that where you got it? Is it clean?"

"These are purified herbs, Edna, grown specifically for teas and other healing products like salves and tinctures."

"What is this supposed to cure?"

"It's for the shrinking of tumours."

"How can tea do that?"

"People don't understand the power of herbs."

"I knew a faith healer named Brother Billy who came to our town every summer when I was a girl. He used herbs for healing, sometimes even snakes. He'd hold up thick leafy branches, wave them in the air above his head." Edna lifted her arms and imitated Billy.

"He'd sweat big moon shapes under his arms and shout for Jesus to anoint him and send healing power into the herbs. Then he'd call out different diseases; cancer of bone, breast and colon, gout, arthritis and what have you. People would raise their hands when their problem was named, and Billy's assistant, with an armful of all kinds of herbs, would hand out the one for the cure. People went home and made teas, believing that Billy's power would turn into liquid healing. I never believed in Billy and if you hadn't helped me in the yard I wouldn't be sitting here drinking this tea now. Dr. Snow, the local doctor, who delivered babies and took care of everyone young and old, said the herbs already had power. They didn't need Brother Billy."

Luna took a sip of tea. "Was anyone actually healed?"

"Oh, some people said they were, but I was suspicious. Billy could have planted them in the audience."

"Herbs do have their own power but the person who handles them can add to or diminish their potency."

"This smells awful." Edna pursed her lips, blew on the

liquid and took a sip of the dark greenish brown tea. "Oh! The taste is bad." She stuck out her tongue and scrunched up her eyes. "Can I add sugar?"

"Adding any kind of sweetener will destroy the effect."

"I'm sorry to hear that."

"Drink some more. It will help you."

"Can I have a bourbon chaser?"

Luna laughed. "What do you think? I'm going to leave the Chaparral with you. You saw how I prepared it. Drink a pot every day. And no bourbon."

There's no way I'm giving up bourbon for this lousy tea, thought Edna, grimacing as she took another sip. "Luna. That's an unusual name. How did your mother decide on it?"

"She didn't. I changed it. She didn't know who I was."

"Doesn't a mother always know her child?"

"Mine didn't."

"How do you know about herbs and whatever it is you did to me last week?"

"Years of study."

Edna noticed that Luna wore an ankle bracelet and another huge ring with what looked like the body of a naked woman on the front. "Is that one of those goddesses you mentioned?"

"Yes. This is Sophia." Luna moved her slender hand toward Edna so she could get a better look.

Luna's gaze stayed steady on Edna as if she was trying to make something happen with her eyes. Maybe she was some kind of witch. Edna pulled the top of her robe across her chest and wondered what she'd gotten herself into. She could use a shot of bourbon. "Where do you live?"

"Papago Trailer Park."

"Oh, my." Edna had never known anyone who lived in a trailer. "Is it safe?"

"Oh, yes, and I have my dog, Tula. It's just temporary until I get on my feet. I moved here two months ago from Wickenburg." Luna poured more tea.

"I drove to Wickenburg once. To blow the carbon out of the car. My husband taught me to do that."

"I had to get out of there. The people are so narrow-minded. I felt like my skin was shrinking up. Know what I mean?"

Edna did know what she meant. She felt like that herself: like she was drying up little by little. Luna reminded Edna of other people she'd met in the barren dryness of this desert town; strange and stubborn like the saguaro cactus that seemed to grow strictly out of an insistence to be alive, or the tenacious weeds that pushed through cracked earth, desert floors, rocks and the Indian caves that Hank used to show her pictures of in *Arizona Highways*. The longer she lived here the more she felt like one of them.

Edna felt fluid leak out of her vagina. "Oh, dear."

"Something wrong?"

"Spotting. Dr. Mann says I need a hysterectomy. I don't want it. I don't trust him. "

"Our bodies belong to us. We're going to reclaim your uterus, Edna."

"We are?"

"Everyone comes into this world with their head between a woman's legs. Think about that.

First, we have to clear this house. Who lived here with you?"

"My husband, Hank."

"It's time to say good-bye." Luna handed Edna an Indian bell. She lit bundles of cedar and sage. They started in the kitchen and wandered from room to room, ringing bells, as Luna waved smoky sticks through the air.

So what if Luna was a witch. Maybe if she followed her instructions, she wouldn't have to be cut open. What did she have to lose?

"I hope this doesn't ruin the wallpaper," said Edna. "It's linen, you know."

When they got to the bedroom Edna stopped ringing. She picked up a photo album from the dresser and showed Luna the pictures.

It looked as if Edna had had a marvellous life with Hank and in the beginning she did; sitting in supper clubs with a big mouthed smile on her face, or dancing and eating "two fingered poi" at luaus in Honolulu with a ring of thick sweet flowers around her head. But after a few years, she'd had to drink to look that happy. She couldn't remember if that was before or after the miscarriage.

Luna closed the album.

"I wish he hadn't died so soon. He wasn't perfect, but I miss him. Sometimes I wish I'd gone with him."

"I know. Ring the bell, Edna." Luna walked around the bedroom making sure the cleansing smoke hit every corner.

"I still have all the love letters he wrote me before we were married. He was very poetic back then."

"We should burn them."

"Oh, no! I couldn't."

"Where are the letters?"

"In the closet, but…"

"Don't worry." Luna put her arm around Edna. " I'm just going to sage them and when you're ready we'll burn them as an offering to Hank's spirit. It's not about destroying anything."

After Luna was satisfied the bedroom was cleared, she led Edna back down the hallway to sage the living room.

Edna made a crunching sound as she sat on the plastic-covered sofa. Luna waved the sticks around until the whole room was thick with smoke. Edna began to cough. "Isn't that enough?"

"There's a lot of energy to clear but we can do the rest another time." Luna sat beside Edna. She turned the sage sticks upside down, ground out the glowing ends in the ashtray on the table.

"That's not an ashtray."

"Oh, I'm sorry. What is it?"

"A crystal candy dish. It's all right. I can't imagine serving candy to anyone again. Were you ever married?"

"Briefly. He was an airline pilot."

"Where did you meet?"

"I was a student at massage school. He was in training and came in for massages to help with stress. After we were married he tried to change me into a conservative trophy wife. He even hired a personal shopper to dress me for the part. But I was more of a tomboy, good at sports when I was younger, especially volleyball. I liked to hike and climb trees, especially ones I wasn't familiar with. I inherited my love of the outdoors from my father."

"Hank was a self-made man. He left the furniture

store his family owned. He disagreed with how his brother managed the place. The store went into bankruptcy a year after we were married. We struggled for a while, but he borrowed some money and started what turned out to be a very successful trucking business. He retired in his early fifties. Hank was so generous. He put some of his relatives through college. And before the polio vaccine came out, he wanted to buy an island and take everyone he knew there, for protection. He had crazy ideas like that. I think I always wanted to be like him. Do you miss your husband?"

"I did at first. I wasn't used to being alone."

"What about children?"

"I'd like that."

Edna saw a flicker of sadness sweep across Luna's face. The crow's feet around her eyes seemed to deepen.

"But if it doesn't happen, children are only one form of creativity. Look at nature."

"I never thought of it that way."

"I want you to do a drawing of your uterus. " Luna took out a drawing pad and package of crayons from her straw basket.

"What? I don't know how to do that."

"I'll do one too. Think about how yours feels inside. What colour is it?" Luna scattered the crayons over the glass coffee table. She chose pink and green and began drawing.

Edna picked red and black. She drew two uneven circles and tentatively filled them in. Her breath became audible. The newsprint started to rip. She drew back and forth harder and harder inside and outside the lines of the circles, a crayon in each of her hands. When the paper ripped in half, she stopped. With the sticks still in her hands, she leaned back into sticky plastic and closed her eyes.

"Very good," said Luna.

Edna sat up and looked at her drawing. "If this is supposed to be my uterus, it looks diseased. Yours is so pretty except for that brown spot in the middle."

A sliver of light glinted off the gold metal fireplace tools. Luna looked out the window and saw a man peering in.

"Do you know him?"

Edna turned. "Oh, that's Joe, the handyman. I forgot all about him."

Joe took off his shirt. White strands of hair on the sides of his head had matted down from sweat. He filled a glass with ice and water, gulped it down. "What is that God awful smell? I've been out there for over an hour. I could have died of heat stroke. The air-conditioner in my car doesn't work. And that Mary across the street kept peeking out her window at me."

"It's fall. It's not that hot. Why didn't you just come in?" Edna tightened the sash of her robe.

"What's all this smoke? You been smoking marijuana?"

"It's sage. It clears negative energy."

"For Christ's sake." Joe lit a cigarette, picked pieces of tobacco off his tongue. "I didn't want to interrupt. I saw a strange car in the driveway, thought maybe it was one of your relatives or maybe another man. I didn't know what to do. Have you seen that car? Once I looked inside I knew it belonged to a woman: shells and feathers and who knows what hanging from the rear-view mirror. The tires are practically bald. The dashboard is covered with some kind of cloth. There's a dog dish on the passenger seat."

"So what? Your car isn't exactly a dream."

"I saw her leave through the breezeway. Who is she?"

"A friend of mine."

"I never saw her before. What's her name? What does she do?"

"Luna. She's a healer. We did drawings of our uteruses. Luna's was pink and moist. Mine looked diseased."

"Oh, for Christ's sake."

"That sounds like something Hank would say."

"I'm sure he wouldn't approve of… what's her name?"

"Luna. Maybe not but he's not here, not even his energy. Luna and I cleared the house and I could clear you too." Edna brought a plate of lemon cake squares to the table, set it down with a thud. "Here, have a piece."

"Don't mind if I do." Joe put his cigarette in the ashtray and took a bite, crumbs sticking in the hair above his lip. "What did you say you did? Cleared something?"

"Never mind."

"I'm just trying to watch out for you like I did when the burglars broke in. Remember? What about the doctor? Aren't you going to have the surgery?"

"Maybe, maybe not."

"If you believe this kook can help you maybe she can, but she could be after more than you realize."

"Like what? Money? I already thought of that. I could say the same about you."

"Me? I'm the one who's been working like a dog around here, for very little money. I've even tried to offer you some physical closeness because whether you admit it or not, you need that."

"You're the one who wants that."

"What can she give you that I can't? Or maybe you've turned lesbian. I've heard about older women who do."

"Don't be ridiculous. I'm going to change my clothes." In the bedroom, Edna thought of the time she worked for Mr. Hodson, the owner of the bookstore in New Castle. He hired her after they had sex that afternoon in the hotel room. She didn't remember his first name. She always called him Mr. Hodson, even in the bedroom. They slept together one other time after he took her to dinner on her birthday. He hired another girl named Lily who had a big bust and red hair, like Edna. Every time Lily or Edna climbed the fifteen-foot ladder to reach the highest strata of shelves for a book, Mr. Hodson would stand underneath, look up their skirts, and try to slip his hand up their legs as they came down the rungs. Lily was prettier than Edna. At first Edna felt jealous, but after a few months working together, they became friends and made a pact to distract Mr. Hodson when either of them went up the ladder.

One day, Edna caught Mr. Hodson kissing Lily in the stock room, with his hand over her silk-covered breast. He snapped at Edna, told her to mind her own business, gave her two week's notice and left the room.

"Why'd you let him kiss you?"

"I need to keep the job." Then Lily put Edna's hand on the same breast and kissed her on the mouth.

Edna didn't feel attracted to her in that way. It felt like kissing herself.

She still couldn't believe Joe had tried to put her hand on his limp penis in the swimming pool. It must be more difficult for men to grow older. She'd been in awe of Hank's confidence, success and financial power. She wondered how he would have changed after he couldn't get it up anymore and if there were Masonic rituals for the penises of old men.

Edna put on a pair of Capri pants with a short sleeve camp shirt, both of which needed ironing. She walked back to the kitchen thinking she'd have to remember to buy more no-iron clothes.

"I'm going out to work on the windbreaker," said Joe.

"You do that. By the way, when will it be finished?"

On her next visit to Edna's, Luna brought Tula. "I hope you don't mind. She'd love to run around in your back-yard."

"I guess that'd be okay."

Tula bolted out the back door and raced through the grass under the magnolia and orange trees. She lapped up pool water, then lay down on the top step, smiling, back legs splayed out behind her.

Edna worried about dog hair clogging the drain but she didn't say anything. Luna and the dog were so happy. They must feel cooped up in that trailer. If the dog hair caused a problem the pool boy could probably fix it.

"Have you been drinking your tea?"

"Every other day is about all I can handle."

"We should finish clearing the house. Let's go to the living room. "

Edna pulled the plastic off the sofa and they sat down.

"There's another spirit in this house besides Hank. A female. Who is it?"

"I don't know."

"Could it be your baby?"

"That happened in Chicago."

"Come down on the floor with me."

Oh, boy. What next? "Do I have to?"

"It would be best."

Edna lay down on the Persian rug in front of the fireplace. Luna sat cross-legged beside her.

"Did you name her?"

"Emma."

"That could be the problem."

"Why?"

Luna put the side of her head on Edna's belly and started to breathe like wind blowing through a canyon.

"What are you doing?"

"Just shifting energy."

Edna remembered how quickly she bloated up when she was pregnant. It was like an alien had attached itself inside her body, gripped her womb like a suckerfish desperate for food. Hank said she looked beautiful. Her breasts had never hurt so much. When Edna complained to Pat, a woman from the Eastern Star bowling league and mother of four, she told Edna to start roughing up her nipples with a towel several times a day to get ready for nursing. "Believe me," she said, "you don't want sensitive nipples." Edna felt physically relieved when it ended. She'd been terrified to be a mother. What if she lost control and hit the child, like her own mother? And if she really was illegitimate, Emma might have been born with abnormal genes.

"Emma's confused," said Luna. "She never got the message that she needed to find another womb."

"I didn't know I was supposed to tell her that. Oh, I feel some cramping."

"In giving her a name she got the idea she was supposed to be with you."

"Oh, dear. I didn't know." Edna let out a small cry.

"It's okay. We'll tell her now." Luna rang a bell over Edna's pelvis. "Emma, you're in a dream boat."

Edna cried out again.

"Emma, it's okay to leave. Go where you can be born and live your dream."

Edna sat up slowly.

"How's the pain?"

"It seems to be gone for now."

"We need to do a 21-day letting go of grief ritual to help you release Emma, Hank and whoever else you're grieving."

"Well okay, but if you're going to keep coming I should pay you. I'm not sure I can afford it. How much do you charge?"

"You can send a check to 'Darryl' in whatever amount you feel is appropriate. I owe him some money. I'll give you his address."

"I have no idea what would be a good amount."

"Whatever you feel is right."

"Well, okay." She'd have to think of someone to ask. Maybe Rose. "What's Darryl's last name?"

"I don't know but it'll get to him."

"I'll do it tomorrow. I feel so tired."

"Let's rest."

The two women went outside and lay on their backs in the afternoon sun. A crisp desert breeze lifted grass smells to their faces and made eddies in the swimming pool water. Tula slept in dirt under the shaded rose bushes.

"We should go to Sedona sometime. There's still good healing energy there even though those resorts are built on Navajo burial grounds. The ancestors are trapped under those tennis courts. Maybe when it starts to snow. All the tourists will be gone. Look, Edna. The tree is making shapes for us. See?" Luna pointed to the left side of the magnolia tree. "There's a snake. And over there, a rooster and a cat."

"I see the snake." Edna turned toward Luna. "Do you have any experience with snakes?"

"I had one when I was a kid. Her name was Strawberry. She looked like a copperhead but she was a Creamsicle corn snake, very gentle. She lived in a big Plexiglas box. I could see every move she made. I'd take her out every day and let her wind around my arm. She liked that."

"Brother Billy used to let those rattlesnakes wind around his body. It made me dizzy. Sometimes he'd hold them in his mouth. Did you ever use your snake for healing purposes?"

"For that you have to handle poisonous snakes and never get bitten so that people will believe in you as a healer. It takes a big ego."

"Billy had that and no one was ever bored at his services." Edna rolled onto her stomach. "I could make us some dinner. I have stuffed green peppers."

A lizard scurried from the grass onto the ochre and sand coloured flagstones. It hovered at the edge of the pool, then disappeared.

Edna didn't recognize them through the peephole. Two massive foreheads loomed large through the magnified glass. She didn't answer but they kept ringing the bell.

"Who is it?" she said through the intercom.

One of them put his eye up to the tiny disc of glass, making prismatic darkness on the other side of the door. Edna jumped back, startled. She tiptoed up to the peephole again. They had backed away. They looked confused, twisting their heads from side to side and over their shoulders, evidently searching for where the voice had come from. Finally, one of them put his mouth next to the intercom box, breathed into it and said in a high whispery voice, "Stewart."

Then Edna saw her sister, Flo. She'd been hiding behind her alien-looking twins. "We came to pay our respects, you know about Hank," she yelled out.

What crap, thought Edna. She opened the door. "It's been almost a year."

"We just couldn't get here until now."

"And you couldn't call?"

"Oh, Edney, don't be mad. We're here now. You poor thing, losing Hank like that."

Edna hadn't seen them since their mother, Bess, died. The boys must be fifty years old now. Stewart, the strangest looking of the two sat next to her at the kitchen table. He looks like he could murder someone, thought Edna. She scooted her chair some inches away. With a blank look, Steven fingered the hula girl salt and pepper shakers that Hank had bought on their first trip to Honolulu. He laid them on their sides and rolled them, as salt and pepper spilled out.

"Stop that," said Edna.

Flo put her hand over Steven's. "This is quite a house you've got here, Edney. Let's have a tour."

"Please don't call me that."

"What's the matter? Too good for your farm name, Edney Mae?"

<hr />

Edna's mother called her Edney Mae when she went on a rampage with the hairbrush. "Oh, Edney Mae. Where are you? Mommy has something for you. Come out. Come out." Edna tried different hiding places, the best was in the barn with the mink, but the more time it took for her mother to find her, the worse the beating. One time, Bess came looking for her daughter in the barn. From behind three deep mink cages, Edna saw her open one and pet the mink named Manny. She picked him up, called him sweetie and made cooing noises. Her mouth touched his fur. Edna had never seen such a thing.

Later, when Bess died, Edna spent days uncontrollably crying out, "Mommy, Mommy," wanting to bring her mother back, try one more time to do whatever was required to be like the finger-size baby mink, Manny. When she cleared out the house, she found boxes of stool softeners and old dirty make-up brushes. Most of Bess' clothes had stains on the front. She wondered what had happened to her mother's smell. She must have stopped wearing the lavender toilet water. Edna looked for secret letters in the dresser underneath Bess' bras, her flowered flannel nightgowns; the wooden box, half full of modest costume jewellery, coat pockets and her mother's four handbags. Edna found tiny safety pins, old potpourri in a lace handkerchief, a dime, a piece of tissue, a red crushed hard candy still in its wrapper, and the wooden handled hairbrush.

Edna never told her father what went on when he wasn't home. She knew if he'd tried to stop it, Bess would have made things worse. After he died, the beatings stopped. Edna was thirteen.

That was the end but the expectation didn't leave her. Every time Hank raised his voice she thought his fist would follow. It never did, but all the beatings were stored somewhere deep in her stomach in what she imagined as a square-shaped box.

Now, Edna led Flo and the twins down the hallway. Steven ran his hand along the linen wallpaper. Stewart mimicked him.

"I hope their hands are clean," said Edna.

"Look at the size of this bedroom. You must be lonely in here all by yourself."

"Not really." Edna knew her sister wanted something. Probably money. This was the buttering up phase before she actually asked.

While Flo and Edna were in the bedroom, the boys

opened the walk-in closet in the dressing area, took out Edna's full-length mink coat and fox stole, put them on, and came into the bedroom giggling, twirling and posing as if they were on a runway. Flo laughed.

"Take those coats off immediately," Edna said. "Flo, if you don't control them you'll have to leave."

"Hand them over," said Flo. Still laughing she laid the furs on the bed. "Let's go see the pool."

"Then will you tell me why you're here?"

"I told you. To pay our respects."

"That's crap and you know it."

They went outside, sat under the umbrella by the unfinished windbreaker. That Joe, thought Edna. He's so slow. Now was the time she needed protection from the crisp fall morning and evening breezes.

"Why don't you boys take a dip while your mother and I talk? The pool is heated. Hank's old swim trunks are in the laundry room. You can change in there."

"Oh, they never got the hang of swimming. We tried. They don't like water."

The twins, with their wispy wheat coloured hair combed over their melon-shaped heads, dressed in white, including suspenders and shoes, reminded Edna of Brother Billy's favourite snake, an albino that used to slither over his body as he undulated with its rhythm. But unlike Billy, his sons were stiff in their movements, as if they'd undergone taxidermy.

When Edna and Flo's father was alive, he forbade his wife and daughters to step foot inside the tattered white tent that was set up every August in a barren field on the Wiley's farm. Soil mulching earthworms sometimes rose up from under the top layer of dry dirt and nibbled at the worshippers toes. Crickets and mosquitoes came out buzzing when the night got thick and damp.

Bess never showed any interest in going, but Edna and Flo liked to sit in the back row. Melvin, Billy's aide who had bad posture and acne, but was adept at catching people when they fainted from being penetrated with spirit, gave the girls the free paper fans that everyone used to cool their faces. When spread out, the fans revealed the words JESUS SAVES in gold letters. Tiny red-eyed snakes were painted below. The colours glinted through the tent like a hundred fireflies trapped in a jar.

Edna and Flo made fun of Billy, all sweaty with his bowl-shaped hair cut, buzzed around his ears and the back of his head, the top an unruly mass of strawberry curls that flopped in his face as he strutted around in front of the make-shift altar; a television stand covered with lace, a vase of wilting white lilies bending low, touching the pages of Billy's opened bible.

The girls were sure he wore make-up. One day, they took a seat near the altar to get a closer look. He preached about his childhood, said he'd grown up in a wealthy family that had intermarried. As the morning wore on, Billy's foundation and black eyeliner melted and streaked down his face.

"He looks like ordinary white trash to me," Flo said to Edna. They giggled behind their fans.

"Most of my family went crazy but I was blessed. Some healing gene got activated. It came upon me at the age of seven when I brought my dog, Snappy, back to life."

Billy would talk about the evil years he spent as a lounge singer and then go into his immortal talk. His eyes glazed over and turned black. "The biggest cult on this planet is the cult of death. We have deathless bodies, just like Jesus. Break your appointment with death and follow me."

The audience shouted "Praise God." Some people stood, arms shot up, hands waved. Edna nudged her elbow at Flo's ribs. They rolled their eyes at each other and laughed.

One Sunday, everything changed. Billy was calling people up to the altar. He pointed at Edna. "You, little lady, with the red hair. Come on up." The way he smiled felt like he was flirting with her. Edna shook her head. The group clapped, egged her on, but she was afraid. She kept her head down and didn't move. Billy turned to Flo. "How about you, Missy?"

"I'm going up to see what it's like."

"Don't do it," said Edna.

"It'll be fun." Flo stood up, started walking toward the altar. Halfway down she turned back and winked at Edna.

Flo didn't faint or fall back into Billy's arms like the others. She could hardly keep from laughing, but that night Edna and Flo went back to the tent to watch Billy handle the snakes. He hadn't done it in public before and he promised miracle healings for everyone who came.

Billy ripped off his shirt, buttons went flying. People in the front row picked through the dirt floor to find one. Melvin appeared at the side of the tent carrying a white wicker cage that moved from side to side as he walked. The top was covered with a shiny purple cloth. Billy whipped it off dramatically, waved it in the air, spoke some words in a strange tongue, and draped the cloth across the open Bible. Then he picked an albino snake and two rattlers from the cage. They wound around his arms, and twisted up and down his torso in so many directions Edna's head began to spin. She thought for sure she would vomit right there in front of everyone. Billy's body glistened, like snake scales.

Flo went wild. She ran to the altar. She began to move like Billy. The albino crawled around her neck, down between her breasts. Edna stood up and screamed. Flo and Billy were in a trance. Nothing could touch them.

They left together after the service. Edna looked for her sister outside, walked around the tent in circles. After a while she heard voices, saw Billy pounding himself against Flo's body, the two of them curved like reptiles up against the side of Billy's silver "Jesus Saves" bus. Flo's skirt was lifted. Billy's pants were at his ankles. Edna had never seen such a thing. She ran home through the dark night as a slice of moon rose above her.

Three months later, in November, Flo started to gain weight. At first everyone thought it was the buttermilk she'd been craving. She drank it straight from the carton. But then came the early morning vomiting. Edna thought Flo would have hell to pay, but Bess became quiet and distant. She never talked about the crazy snake-handling preacher who had knocked up her daughter.

Six months later, twin boys slid out of Flo. Dr. Snow said he'd never seen such an easy birth. They were alien-looking babies, on the verge of deformity; with thin almost absent lips and deep-set eyes like caverns in outer space.

Flo told Edna that when she had sex with Billy, God penetrated her.

"Maybe that's how it feels with everyone. You never did it before."

"No. It was God. Billy said so and I could feel it."

If Edna hadn't been so afraid of Billy she might have had the twins instead of Flo. She was his first choice. She could have been stuck on the farm and never met Hank.

Billy didn't come back to New Castle. Flo tried to find him one summer in Virginia. She'd heard he was preaching there.

The boys didn't make a sound until they were two, but at age six they started to sing in pitch-perfect high crystalline voices. Their throats vibrated with a melancholy sweetness.

Over the years, Flo sent Edna pictures of the boys. As teenagers they looked like larger alien babies. In each photo, their pants were too short, pulled up high in the crotch as if they had no penises. They wore suspenders and barbershop quartet armbands. Singing was the only job they could get. Hank paid for singing lessons when they were children so they'd always have something to count on. When they grew older, Flo sent them to Bible school to learn to preach, but they weren't articulate. They didn't have Billy's gift or his looks. Billy's inbreeding had caught up to his children.

"Five thousand should do it," said Flo. "It's for work, Edney. The American consulate in Austria contacted the boys. I saw an ad in an international singing magazine for a job with a famous Austrian choir. I sent in a tape and the boys were chosen to audition. They need money for plane fare and travel expenses. It's a lifetime opportunity."

"Lifetime opportunity," the boys said in unison.

Flo leaned across the table under the shade of the umbrella. "They still sing like angels, Edney. You remember. It's all they know. How will they survive when I'm gone? Barbershop quartet jobs are scarce these days. This is their last chance for a secure future. If they get in, they're guaranteed a yearly salary and benefits."

"What makes you think I have that kind of money?"

"Are you kidding? Look at this place. Hank must have left you a fortune."

"That's not true. In fact, I need surgery. I might need special care. I'll need every dime. Insurance doesn't cover everything. Or I could live to be a hundred like Aunt Clara. I don't have enough money to last that long."

"I could stay on and take care of you."

"No, thank you."

"What's another five thousand? It won't make or break you. We're family."

"Really. And where have you been all these years? Hank never heard a thank you for the singing lessons."

A lizard ran past Steven's foot. "Help!" He turned to his mother, lifting his feet up, trying to fold his legs underneath him, but he didn't have the flexibility.

Flo patted his arm. "It's gone now, honey."

Steven's hands shook as he tried to hold his legs up off the ground.

"Lifetime opportunity," Stewart said, rubbing his hands up and down the umbrella pole.

"These boys are the light of my life. I don't know who I'd be without them. When I count my blessings I count each one of them three times."

"That sounds like something you read on a greeting card."

"Well, look at you, all alone in your old age."

Edna put her shoulders back in spite of a cramping sensation. "At least I got married and had a life. You had no prospects with those boys as part of the package. Maybe you can find their father. He should help."

"I thought you knew. Billy died a few years ago."

"He's dead?"

"It was a snake bite to the throat. Poor thing was never bitten until he had to commercialize himself. He had no choice. All those churches got built. No one wanted to sit in a hot tent anymore and Billy wasn't the type to preach in a regular church. His donations dwindled. The deadly bite happened on television. Everyone saw it. What a terrible humiliation, to end like that after all the people he helped."

Edna started to perspire under her arms and between her legs. She felt a twinge in her uterus. She leaned forward, held her belly.

"He had this see-through bathtub made so people could get a good look at the snakes. He'd get in there with eighty-seven of them, a world record. He'd lie real still. He couldn't move with them like he used to. Spirit wouldn't protect him anymore. This was a show, not a healing. He had to follow natural laws, which say you have to be still around snakes or they'll bite you."

Edna went to the pool, sat on the edge and dangled her feet in the water. The square box in her stomach tightened. She lowered her body all the way in, swam to the centre of the deep end and began to float on her back. She remembered her mother's terror of water. Bess wouldn't go near it.

Flo came to the edge of the pool. "Edney, what are you doing? Come out of there. We can't swim. Are you all right?"

Edna couldn't hear her. She was lost in a memory, locked away until now. Years ago, Bess instructed Edna to stay home and take care of Flo, who was sick with the flu, while she went out shopping. But Edna got bored. She went to Billy's tent, sat in back as usual. She was shocked to see her mother sitting in the front row. When Billy called for people to come to the altar and be saved, Bess jumped up. She ran into Billy's arms sobbing. Edna could tell this wasn't the first time.

Now, Edna felt dizzy. A tightly coiled piece of her mind started to spin and unwind. She put her hand on her forehead.

"Edney. Come out of there," yelled Flo, holding onto the pool ladder.

That night on the porch, Edna lay awake in her daybed as her brain made fresh grooves, reconfiguring lifelong doubt and confusion. If Emma had lived, she might have been just like the twins, or worse. Nature did know best.

Flo slept in the bedroom, the boys in the guest room. Edna thought of calling Joe for advice about giving Flo the money, but she knew he'd say not to. She went with what she knew Hank would do. At four in the morning she got up and wrote a check, left it on the kitchen table, went back to bed and fell asleep. Three hours later the phone rang. There'd been an accident.

A semi-truck had hit Flo's beat up car as she tried to get on the freeway. The policeman said it looked as though the car couldn't accelerate fast enough to get ahead of the truck. "Bad timing," he said.

Steven survived, but his legs were crushed. Before he arrived at St. Joe's hospital, he went into a coma. Edna sat by his bed that first day feeling numb except for the occasional pain in her pelvis. There was no way Luna's smoking sticks and teas could uncrush Steven's legs. He wouldn't walk again. Edna felt the weight of his care press down on her neck. At least Flo died with some hope for the boys: Edna's nephews and, now she knew, her half-brothers as well.

She realized that with the exception of Steven, she was bereft of blood relatives. It didn't matter that she hadn't been close to Flo or that she'd hardly known Steven and Stewart, she now experienced a floating sensation, as if she might drift off the earth. Edna gripped the bars on Steven's hospital bed as if to anchor herself. She studied his face, tried to find her own. Instead, she saw the face of Billy, angelic and alien. If he were alive, she'd probably try to find him. Who had his parents been? Who and what was she orphaned from?

Edna visited Steven every week until he finally woke up two months later. He became agitated when he saw her, needed shots of morphine to calm him down. He had no idea who she was.

Edna moved him to Sunnyslope Palms. Gwen came

up with the idea to wheel Steven into the chapel for Sunday church services so he could perform one or two musically difficult hymns and then lead the congregation in singing the more ordinary ones.

Since the accident, Edna hadn't been able to sleep. She had no interest in solitaire. The thought of it brought on heavy sighs. One day, she put on her bathing suit, sat at the kitchen table and stared out the window at the pool. If I go in I'll drown, she thought. Cool blue water had become a source of fear.

When Joe came over, Edna tried to act normal, faked her usual routine, including laying out cards as if she had a game going. Inside, she felt like one of Billy's snakes: undulating like crazy, as if trying to swallow a half live, still bucking wild mustang. Her body couldn't assimilate the loss of her family, the truth about Billy and the fact that she would die alone. Her uterus and digestive tract, constipated with death, rumbled, ached, and cramped. A hoof stuck in her throat, a knee joint in her stomach, a flank in her pelvis. Bourbon didn't help and neither did Valium.

She hoped she would just drop dead (no wasting away at Sunnyslope Palms), maybe in the market; at the beauty shop, preferably after Rose had coloured her hair; in a car accident like Flo, or in the backyard under the magnolia tree. Fermin would find her. He'd say a Catholic prayer in Spanish. Edna liked that idea.

One morning, Edna woke from a deep sleep to the sound of the backdoor slamming. It must have been 8:00, Joe's usual time to come in the house after working on the windbreaker. She hadn't made coffee or the breakfast snacks she typically had waiting for him. He called her name but she couldn't answer. She was barely conscious, lying on the Persian rug in front of the fireplace on the living room floor, wetness surrounding her hips. Soon, he was standing over her in a panic.

In the emergency room, Dr. Mann told Joe that Edna would bleed to death if he didn't do the hysterectomy. When it was over, Joe sat at Edna's bedside, waited for her to wake up.

Her filmy eyes squinted open. "Oh, it's you. Where's Hank? Where am I?"

"St. Joe's."

"This is where Hank died. Get me out of here." She tried to pull herself up. "Oh, dear. I can't. I have so much pain."

"I can adjust the bed. You just had surgery."

"What? Who did that?"

"Your doctor."

"What doctor? I didn't give permission."

"Calm down. Dr. Mann. The only doctor listed in your appointment book. It had to be done to save your life."

"That's crap. I'll sue the son of a bitch. Where's Luna?"

"A lot of good that spook did you."

"Her number is in my address book in my purse. Where did they put my bag? Go get the nurse. Someone probably stole my wallet. Look in that cabinet. Oh, it's there on the chair."

"I know. That's where it's been all along. How do you think we found Dr. Mann's number?"

"I could kill him. Do you see Luna's number? It's under L?"

"I'll find it." Joe sat down with Edna's purse on his lap. "Go back to sleep."

"I'm in too much pain. That bag looks so worn out."

Dr. Mann swaggered into the room with his big whitened teeth showing. "How's our girl doing?" he said to Joe. His duck tie grazed Edna's hospital gown as he leaned in and patted her arm. He seemed shorter or maybe he was fatter than the last time she'd seen him. Edna pulled her arm away. "I should sue you."

Dr. Mann's teeth suddenly disappeared. "Now, now," he said, turning to Joe. "I warned her if she didn't take care of this there would be problems, but she was lucky. No cancer."

"Talk to me. Not him. He's not my husband. And get me something for this pain. It's killing me."

"I'll take care of it." Dr Mann buzzed for the nurse. "It was touch and go for awhile but I managed to bring her through. Fortunately, I didn't have to do an abdominal. It was a perfect procedure."

"I suppose I should be grateful."

"That would be nice. After all, I was in the middle of a golf game." He looked at Joe and laughed. "I went right through your belly button, Edna, and just ground up your uterus. It's a good thing we got that out of there. And it wasn't easy but I saved the ovaries."

"I'm going to be sick."

"She's cranky, that's all." Joe stood next to Dr. Mann as if they were colleagues.

"You don't know what I am and don't you dare apologize for me. Get me some drugs."

"You'll need someone with you at home for the next few months."

"I can take care of her," said Joe. "As a matter of fact, I have a medical degree from the University of Minnesota. Couldn't get licensed here. Unfortunate circumstances."

"I see. Dr. Mann cleared his throat and patted his tie. Well, Edna, there you go. You have the perfect person."

"We'll see about that. Please get me something for this pain."

"When you recover," said Joe, "I'll take you for an ice cream soda at the old Carnation factory before they shut it down. We can play the jukebox, listen to some Count Bassie."

"Oh, for God's sake. Call Luna."

"Well, I'll leave you two to your plans. I'll check on her in a day or two. And here comes the nurse with your pain medication. Bye bye now."

Edna yelled after him, "Just so you know, I don't believe in shooting ducks."

XIII

Luna sat on the toilet lid, her lanky legs crossed, her right foot jiggling back and forth grazing Tula's fur. The dog had curled herself around the bottom of the toilet. Luna held the pregnancy stick in her left hand and waited. The Milky Way looked unusually creamy as she gazed through the rain-stained skylight that Darryl had put in a year ago to increase the value of the trailer. The bathroom was dark except for tiny specks of light shining through the window and door openings of the Taos Pueblo nightlight.

The stick turned pink. This wasn't the way she planned it.

Luna's vision board didn't include a picture of a single mother, but one of herself standing with a sandy-haired man holding a baby girl in front of a Spanish style house with red bougainvillea framing the arched doorway. She also had a picture of a family of sand crabs, a male, female and two babies. The sand crab became her animal totem one day on a beach in Kauai, where she'd gone for a solar return on her thirtieth birthday. An astrologer told her she'd had a very fertile past life there. While sitting on the beach, a crab sauntered up, the way they do, and stopped in front of her, didn't move for an hour, except to retreat and come out of its shell again and again. Luna started to sob and couldn't stop, nor could she move. Her girlfriend, Peggy, who'd made the trip with her, had to get help from some local beach boys to help Luna to the car. Later, she told Peggy she felt she'd come home and didn't want to return to her husband.

———

Luna had had sex with Darryl one more time after she decided she wouldn't anymore, and once the same week with Mark, a doctor she met on cupidsmatch.com, after their dinner date at the Royal Palms resort, spending the night in one of the casitas with a close-up view of Camelback Mountain.

In bed, Mark told her he appreciated that there'd been no lull in the conversation during dinner. "With a lot of women there's too much awkward silence."

But he didn't call for another date. Luna guessed it was because she didn't drink enough and he felt uncomfortable drinking three cocktails, two bottles of wine with dinner, and a brandy with dessert, compared to her one club soda and half a glass of wine. Or it could have been the heated discussion they had about the validity of anti-depressants; he insisted they were a necessity in today's world with people under so much stress. "Every generation has its problems and new drugs are discovered to deal with them," he said.

Luna argued there were other ways; change in lifestyle, meditation and natural remedies. "What if enough people refused to live lives of debilitating stress?"

"No one has time for that," he said.

Neither of them backed down and that became a turn on, as if sex would have the last word.

During dinner Mark told Luna that before he became a doctor he'd been a bartender at the Rusty Pelican in Marina del Rey, California. His biceps and chest were muscle thick from too much working out. He was shorter than Luna and, like Darryl, wore three-inch high cowboy boots.

She couldn't decide which one she'd rather have be the father. Probably neither. Genetically speaking, her ex-husband would have been best. Practically speaking, she should tell Mark. She had no money and no health insurance, but he probably wouldn't believe the baby was his. If he insisted on a DNA test, it might turn out negative. At thirty-five she wouldn't have an abortion. This was the first time she'd gotten pregnant and it might not happen again.

Luna covered herself with the pink satin quilt from her bed and lay down on the green shag rug she'd bought on sale at the Macy's store near Edna's house. She put her hands on her belly, made deep sounds to connect with the spirit inside, and imagined the fluids in her womb already forming the baby. She knew it was a girl.

The phone rang several times before she got up to answer it.

"Yeah. Uh. This is Joe Wilkes. Edna's friend. We haven't met. Edna's here in the hospital. She keeps asking for you. Can you come to St. Joe's?"

"What happened?"

"I found her bleeding. The doctor did the hysterectomy. I know she didn't want it but..."

"I'll be right there."

When Luna arrived, Edna was sitting up with a tray in front of her. "Look at this crap. It's worse than my Mormon neighbours' food bribes."

Luna sat on the bed and hugged her. She put the side of her head on Edna's chest.

Edna started to cry. "They keep taking blood. Every hour. I have no more veins and they do it anyway. No matter how much pain they cause. These people are inhuman."

"Do some deep breaths, Edna. You have to exhale, breathe out, so I can breathe you in."

"They all died and Billy is my father. The last thing I remember is feeling like I had a big animal inside of me, just filling me up."

Joe cleared his throat, moved closer to the bed.

"Oh, this is Joe," said Edna.

Luna stood up to give him a hug. He stopped her by putting his hand out. "Don't come too close. I smell. I was working outside before I went in the house and found our girl on the living room floor. I used to have heightened powers of smell. I could tell when a woman was menstruating."

"Really?" said Luna.

"He thinks that's a racy thing to say but it's vulgar, vulgar, vulgar! You can go back to the house. I'll be fine now."

"Going to do some mumbo jumbo?" Joe shook his hands in the air around his face and bugged his eyes out. "You girls going to smoke some pot? That's what it's called these days. Right? Don't let the nurses catch you."

Luna went back to Edna and began grabbing the

air above her pelvis, then quickly opening her hands behind her.

"What the hell are you doing?" asked Joe.

"Removing negative energy. Open the door, Joe, so this can get out. And you'd better get out of the way. These are some powerful entities."

"What a spook," he said under his breath.

Luna snapped her head around to look at him. "So I've been told. I have heightened powers of hearing."

"Touché. Well, guess I'm not needed here anymore. Pleasure," he said to Luna. "I'll be back tomorrow, Edna." He shuffled out the door; his right shoulder slumped down further than his left.

"I've had it with him. As soon as he finishes that windbreaker, he's out of the picture."

"If it weren't for him, you might be dead."

"Exactly."

Luna thumbed through a *Reader's Digest*, and at Edna's request, read the titles of articles aloud. Wearing a cream-coloured, silk bed jacket with the letter E monogrammed in pale blue over her heart, Edna said, "Boring. They're all about diseases or food."

Since Edna's return from the hospital, a week ago, Luna had been staying in the guest room. It was twice the size of her teardrop trailer. She slept on one of the thick-mattressed twin beds. The fabric in the centre of the headboards and the draperies was heavy gold-flowered chintz. Her feet sunk into the thick carpeting as if it was fertile soil. The guest bathroom tub was long enough for her body to stretch all the way out. Above the marble countertop and sink, mirrors were angled in every direction.

The first night, after Edna fell asleep, Luna roamed around the house. In the living room, she looked at the Dresden porcelain figurines in curio cabinets, mostly ballerinas and dancing couples wearing hats. She read the plaques on Edna's golf and bowling trophies in the den and imagined herself nursing her baby in the hand-carved rocking chair in the corner. She wondered if Edna had had the same idea when she was pregnant. Luna would have to tell her soon. She was starting to throw up and gain weight.

Tula stayed in the back yard, getting in Joe's way, jumping up on his legs with a ball in her mouth, as he tried to finish the windbreaker.

Edna didn't want to see Joe. She told Luna about the time he tried to have sex in the pool. Luna talked her into letting him in the bedroom occasionally to play double solitaire. She thought it would help her. He was a little creepy but he cared and felt attached to Edna. Luna knew he felt slighted that she was in charge, but they didn't talk about it. Neither of them wanted to create confrontation during Edna's recovery. Joe took his cigarette breaks outside under the magnolia tree or in the kitchen by himself.

"Speaking of food," said Edna, smoothing the bed sheets across her lap, "be a dear and make me a sardine sandwich on that black bread in the fridge. Please. And make one for yourself. Sardines are loaded with protein, you know. And I'll have a slice of chocolate cake and a bourbon."

"The doctor said no drinking."

Edna rolled her eyes. "I hate him. He thinks he's God. When he told me he left my ovaries, he acted like I should bow to him. Rose told me, at my age, the ovaries don't mean diddly-squat. She didn't use that expression. She said something in Spanish I didn't understand, but I knew she meant diddly-squat."

"Ovaries symbolize new beginnings, new growth and fruitfulness. Think about that."

"I'm too old to think about that."

"Maybe the hysterectomy was a good thing. Maybe a piece of Emma remained attached to your uterus all these years. Now you're both completely free, but we still need to do an energetic clearing. And there's the rest of your family. The energy of your incomplete feelings about these people is swirling around inside your body."

"Why bother? I'm very fond of you, dear, and I like having you around, but nothing you've done has worked. I thought you were going to cure me."

"I never said that. It's up to the universe and the laws of nature to work things out for your highest good. Sometimes we don't know why things happen as they do until much later."

"Well, that's a fine kettle of fish."

The doorbell rang and Edna's shoulders jerked. Tula barked from the back yard. "Don't answer. It has to be those Mormons. They've been bothering me since the summer Hank and I moved in. One time, Mary sent her son, Reid, who was only twelve at the time, to the door with a chiffon pie and a large pop-up book showing a scene of Joseph Smith leading his people to the Promised Land."

The doorbell rang again. "Ignore it. They've probably brought a Jell-O mould, a pie or a cake loaded with sugar on a china plate I'll have to return. After Hank died they wanted to do a baptism for the dead so he could accept God's true church and go to the celestial kingdom. Can you believe the nerve? Now they're back for me. When I kick the bucket, promise you won't let them get their hands on me."

Luna took Edna's hand. "I won't and you're not going to kick the bucket anytime soon."

"The universe might have other plans. I'm so tired. Everything you need to know is in my will."

"I'll go check the door."

"Turn off the burglar alarm first."

"It's already off."

The first day Luna came to stay, she learned how to turn the alarm off and on with a code number and a switch inside the closet. She felt claustrophobic when she learned that the windows in the guest room wouldn't open. They were covered with special green-tinted screens that were hooked up to the alarm. The guest room closet was filled with hatboxes. Edna had Luna move them into the master bedroom to make room for her clothes. She asked Luna to open one. Inside was a hat made of coral velvet. "Hank called this one my 'chorus girl' hat." It had feathers that curved up high away from her face. She cocked it at an angle and turned her head from side to side sitting up in bed, modelling for Luna. She suddenly lay back on the pillows. "Oh, I'm so tired."

"It's time to rest," said Luna. "You can show me the hats later."

Luna went to the front door.

"Don't open it no matter who it is."

Luna looked through the peephole. "Whoever it was went away," she called to Edna. She went to the kitchen to make the sardine sandwich and was startled by Joe at the table smoking in his undershirt.

"How is she?"

"Agitated about the Mormons."

"She's afraid of them. She's surrounded on all sides you know. They like this neighbourhood." Joe took a deep drag from his cigarette, blew smoke in Luna's direction.

"I wasn't aware. Does she like mustard or mayo on her

sandwich?" Luna got out the black bread and opened a can of sardines.

"Seems like you should know. Mustard. I hate that smell. Can you do something about your dog? Tie him up when I'm working? I don't have time to play ball."

"Her name is Tula."

"Yeah, whatever." Joe ground out his cigarette and kept grinding as he stood. "Will you do something about the dog?"

"I'll figure something out."

He opened the back door. "Tell Edna I said hello."

Edna was asleep when Luna went back to the bedroom with a tray. She put it on the dresser and sat by the bed. Edna looked younger. The lines in her face seemed to have decreased; some deep tension fell away when she slept. She woke after a few minutes.

"I ran into Joe. He asked about you."

"I want to show you something. Come over to this side of the bed. In case of an emergency..." Edna pulled open the top drawer of the night table. "It's loaded. My gardener, Fermin, got me a good price. Read that note in the drawer."

"Wow. That's scary. It says, '25 calibre Colt automatic pistol.' It's so small."

"It's a woman's gun."

"Have you ever shot it?"

"Not yet."

"Do you know how?"

"How hard could it be? If anyone breaks in, just point and shoot. Do you want to hold it?"

"No. Well, maybe I could touch the mother of pearl handle, but leave it in the drawer." Luna noticed a deck of playing cards next to the gun, printed with the words Don the Beachcomber, Honolulu. Luna rubbed her hand over the shiny opaqueness. "It's so smooth. It's hard to believe something so beautiful could kill someone. It bothers me." Luna put her hands on her belly. "I'm pregnant."

"No kidding. Well, I'll be darned. Who's the father?"

"One of two guys. But they won't be involved."

"That's wonderful, honey. Why didn't you tell me sooner?"

"I just found out last week. In fact it was the day you had surgery."

"Have you seen a doctor?"

"Not yet."

"You have to go right away. I know money is tight so you go and I'll pay for it."

"Oh, no. I couldn't accept that."

"Think of it as payment for taking care of me. How far along are you?"

"Maybe six weeks or so."

Luna closed the drawer. "Anyway, I'd hate to get shot somehow and have something happen to the baby. Tula is a good watchdog. You heard her just now and how she barks when Joe comes around. We can get a Beware of Dog sign. And if we intend not to attract violence…"

"Before I met you I had a burglary in this house. They stole some of my jewellery and dumped Hank's ashes all over the carpet. I just want to feel safe."

"I know. Maybe we could lock it up."

"We'd be dead before we could get to it. A gun can't be any more dangerous than living in a trailer park. We'll figure something out. Let's talk about the baby."

On the day he finished the windbreaker, Luna saw Joe from the kitchen window tape something to the side of the white and yellow structure that curved around the kidney-shaped pool. She knew he missed spending time with Edna and that he'd been dragging his feet, hoping to get back into the house as he'd been before.

Luna found the note that night when she went outside to feed Tula. She read it to Edna. "I was stung by a scorpion today. It's a 'sign,' as Luna would say, that my time here is over. Not that you would worry, but I'm okay. Urine neutralizes the venom so I peed on my hand. Goodbye, Edna. Have a nice rest of your life. Please send my final payment of $100 to my address on Hubbell Street. If you're not up to it maybe Luna can take care of it. Joe."

"Poor thing. What a shame," said Edna.

She'd just finished her favourite TV dinner of Salisbury steak, mashed potatoes and peas. Luna didn't believe in eating TV dinners or meat but Edna insisted on buying several the day before when they went to the market, Edna's first outing since her surgery three weeks ago. She could have bought the best cuts of meat but she said that had been Hank's domain. As usual, Luna tested the vibrations of fruit as Edna held onto the cart with one hand and Luna's arm with the other. They also went to see Dr. Mann that day. Edna's recovery was "right on schedule," he said. Edna badgered him about when she could start having cocktails again.

"It's dangerous to mix liquor with your medications." Dr. Mann put out his hand to help her off the examination table.

"What could happen?" She wrapped the paper sheet around her hips.

"You could have a heart attack or a stroke."

"I'm willing to take the risk." She wouldn't give up, so finally he told her she could have one drink a day if taken with a meal.

"What a control freak," said Edna as Luna helped her into the ten-year-old Honda station wagon. Crystals spun from the rear-view mirror. "If I can have one I can certainly have two. What's the difference?"

Edna had planned to get her hair done that afternoon, but she was too tired to keep the appointment.

Now, Edna downed the one shot of bourbon Luna had put on the tray with the TV dinner.

"Poor Joe," Luna said.

"I'm sorry his feelings were hurt, poor guy, but he couldn't hang around here forever. We have to call the exterminator."

"They use poison."

"Of course they do. We can't have scorpions out there. What if you got stung and it affected the baby. A sting could kill Tula."

"So could that toxic bug spray."

"We have no choice."

"There are other ways. I learned from Darryl. He

has elderly people in the trailer park, allergic to strong poison and the disabled woman got sick once after a spraying. He took me with him on a scorpion hunt. We had to wait for a night with no moon and with a black light we walked around the park looking for them. He wanted to see how many there were, what he was dealing with. We finally found their home, in a pile of old car parts in back of one of the trailers. Did you know they have live births, no eggs? There were thousands of them. They glow at night like neon lights. It was the most beautiful thing I ever saw, like a galaxy of stars on the ground." Luna closed her eyes for a moment, remembering the sight.

"How did he get rid of them?"

"Oh, he got a couple of chickens and a cat. They ate them all."

"Well I'll be darned. I never heard of such a thing and I grew up on a farm. Of course we didn't have scorpions."

"There's some kind of a sound device that drives them away but Darryl didn't trust that that would work. Oh, and peacocks will eat scorpions too but they make a lot of noise and they cost more than chickens or cats."

"I can't have a chicken here in the Palmer Estates. There are rules. Probably not a peacock either. Too bad. They're so pretty. I guess I could get a cat. You'll have to take care of it. But if that doesn't work, I'm calling the exterminator."

Luna took the bed tray from Edna's lap and set it on the night table. The drawer was slightly open. She smelled mahogany. The edge of the gun's mother of pearl handle shone with pale-coloured milky-ness in the lamp's light. She would never try but she wondered if she could figure out how to unload it and hide the bullets. She slid the drawer closed. "You probably don't want me hanging around here forever either, just until you're well."

"You're a different story. You can stay here as long as you like."

Luna sat on the edge of the bed. "I need to decide what to do, where to go now that the baby is coming. I'm almost at three months. I don't want to raise a child in a trailer."

"I agree. What about your mother?"

"I haven't talked to her since my divorce. She thinks I should have stayed no matter what. For her, it's all about having a man. She doesn't approve of my life-style."

Edna didn't approve either but she didn't let on. She patted Luna's hand. She felt a prong on the goddess ring scratch her finger but she didn't move. "Well, what about the father? How many possibilities are there?"

Luna named the two candidates and Edna advised her to call Dr. Mark and tell him the baby was his. "What's his last name?"

"I don't even know."

"It's not a lie. Right now, it's fifty percent true. What-ever you do, don't tell that Darryl anything. You need to get yourself set up financially. You'll want to stay home with the baby. You don't want to have to get a job."

"I'd still want to do my healing work."

"But you can't depend on it to make a living."

Luna lowered her voice as if someone other than Edna was in the room. "I don't know if I like him that much.

It was only one date and he's so into western medicine."

"He's a doctor for God's sake. You can't expect him to go around burning sage. If you like him well enough, at least you'll be secure. Then later if you divorce him he'll have to give you money."

"I didn't picture things this way."

"Honey, no one ever does. I think I should meet him."

Luna thought maybe Edna was right. Her days of risk taking should end. She should make a safe choice, not wait for the perfect one to appear.

Luna found Mark's card at the bottom of her Kachina doll tote bag underneath a pack of tarot cards. She called and left a message hoping he would remember her.

Three days later the phone rang and she knew it was him. "Luna. I think I remember you. Royal Palms, right? And you don't believe in anti-depressants."

"Well, that's not entirely true." Luna thought she'd better tone down her opinions or he would run for the hills.

"Would you like to go out next Saturday night?"

"I'd love to. I wonder if you'd do me a favour. I'm staying with a friend, an older woman who just had a hysterectomy. Her doctor says her recovery is going well."

"Who's her doctor?'

"Dr. Mann."

"Gerontology is my specialty you know."

"Oh, perfect. Would it be too much to ask you to visit with her for a minute before we go out? It would give her a little encouragement."

"I guess I can do that. I'll be there at seven. What's the address?"

Luna would never have let him come to the trailer but Edna's house was a different story.

Luna hadn't left Edna alone since the surgery. She suggested Edna get an emergency pendant in case something happened while she was out with Mark.

"I'm not pressing a button for some stranger. God only knows who might show up."

"You need to trust the universe to bring what you need."

"I guess. After all, you showed up, but I still don't want a pendant. It makes me feel a hundred years old. I'll call 911 if I need help."

"What if you can't get to the phone or can't dial?"

"My intuition tells me nothing is going to happen. How do you like that, Miss Goddess?"

Luna laughed. "Okay then. We'll set up the phone by your bed and leave it at that. I don't use a cell phone so you can't call me. They cause cancer and fry your brain. I'll find out where we're going for dinner and leave that number for you."

"Okay, deary, I like that idea."

Through the peephole, Mark's hair looked too high. Luna hoped it was just magnification but when she opened the door she saw it was not. He had on the same black cowboy boots he'd worn on their first date. The hair and boots gave him height but in an overly obvious way. Did he go to all this trouble during the day for his patients? He wore a body-hugging shirt, a little too tight, so that his nipples stood out. The muscles in his chest were so defined from working out he'd developed small breasts.

Edna would tell her to not be so negative, to think about the baby's future.

"Come in." Luna smiled as big as she could and gave him a hug, feeling her breasts squish into his. She bumped his doctor bag with her thigh. "Wow, that's heavy. I really appreciate your seeing my friend."

"No problem." He looked down at her bare feet.

"Oh, I'm not quite ready yet. I'll take you to meet Edna."

Before he arrived, Edna had Luna bring a tube of red lipstick and a hand mirror to the bed, asked her to arrange a beaded comb in her hair. "On the right. My best side." She had Luna find the chocolate-coloured silk bed jacket with the mink trim. Knowing how Luna would react, Edna told her the mink was fake.

"Well, how do you do," said Edna. "Aren't I lucky to have such a handsome visitor."

Oh, boy, thought Luna. I was right. This kind of attention from a young man would give Edna a boost. "I'll leave you two while I finish getting dressed."

"You go dear. We'll be just fine."

"May I call you Edna?"

"Of course. You know that Luna is a lovely girl."

"Yes, she is." Mark listened to Edna's heart, took her pulse and asked her what Dr. Mann had said about her recovery.

"He said everything was fine, but I don't have much energy."

"That's to be expected at this stage. Luna said you went to the market."

"I ran out of steam and had to come home."

"Do you mind if I press lightly on your belly?"

"Be my guest."

Mark palpated Edna's pelvis through her beige silk nightgown. "Any pain anywhere?"

"No. You have very good hands."

"Everything seems just fine. The tissue around where the uterus used to be takes time to heal and the best thing for healing is rest."

"You're so knowledgeable. You'd make someone a wonderful husband."

"Well, thank you, Edna."

"Do you think I could have a couple of cocktails with dinner?'

"I don't see why not."

Luna appeared in the doorway in a sparkling skirt and flat shoes.

"Don't you look pretty," said Edna.

"Yes, she does." Mark looked at her feet and smiled. "Lovely."

"She's wearing my 1950s Hawaiian skirt, hand beaded by native women in Honolulu. My husband and I used to take cruises there. Those were happy times. Luna liked that skirt so much I told her she could have it. There's not another one like it and I don't have any use for it now."

Mark kissed Edna's hand. "I hope to see you again soon. You take good care of yourself."

"You kids have fun."

Luna went to the night table for a pad and pen.

"Where are we going? I want to leave a number for Edna."

"I thought we'd go to the Royal Palms again. I'll write it down. I have the number in my head. I go there a lot."

Luna kissed Edna on the cheek. The mink trim brushed her face. "Are you sure that's fake? It feels too soft."

"Oh, I'm sure." She winked at Luna and whispered, "He's a good catch, honey."

"Shall we go?" Mark offered his arm.

Luna liked how he attended to Edna. He had a great bedside manner. That's how he'd be with the baby. She wondered if she should tell him tonight.

The valet at the Royal Palms opened the passenger door of Mark's black BMW and with a sweep of his arm bowed slightly as Luna's sparkling sandals—she'd glued multicoloured rhinestones to the straps to match Edna's Hawaiian skirt—stepped onto the flagstone driveway. She probably should have polished her toenails for the occasion, but she hated nail polish, felt trapped behind it, sealed off, her whole body airless.

She and Mark strolled down the pathway that led to the restaurant's iron double doors. They walked through a fragrant citrus grove with blooming flowers and a cactus garden of pear, yucca and mutated saguaro. The resort had the feel of a private residence and Luna thought it wouldn't be so bad to live with this kind of luxury.

They were seated next to a huge stone fireplace, surrounded by European antiques, tiles and artefacts. Luna stared into the fire, asked for its wisdom to guide the evening.

"You seem different from the last time we went out," said Mark.

He looked better in dim light; his jaw became more square as fire flames and candlelight made shadows across his face, giving him a chiselled look.

"I can't put my finger on it. I remember you don't drink."

Now I have a reason you would understand, Luna thought. She should have a drink to make him more comfortable. One probably wouldn't hurt anything. "Maybe I'll have a drink later or wine with dinner."

Mark ordered Scotch on the rocks, Luna, club soda.

"How'd you meet Edna?"

"In the market."

"She's quite a character."

"Oh, yes."

"She seems perfectly fine by the way." Mark finished his scotch, signalled the waiter for another.

"That's a relief. Thank you so much for taking a look at her. I didn't know you specialized in geriatrics. That must be so rewarding."

"Well yes, and it's very lucrative. Everyone gets old. Do you live there with Edna?"

"Temporarily."

"And permanently?"

"An apartment near there. And you?"

"A townhouse in the Judson Estates in Paradise Valley. Judson was a private school for sixty years. It's a shame they had to tear it down, but everything has to change eventually, have to make room for the new. Right?"

"Sometimes new isn't for the better."

"That may be, but it doesn't stop happening."

"One can fight it." Watch it, Luna thought, or this would end up like last time when they argued about anti-depressants for the entire evening. "Let's order dinner. What's good?"

"The strip steak is excellent. Or the lamb chops."

Luna grew up eating meat but had stopped after she heard the Indian men chanting at Montezuma's Castle. She ordered scallops, hoping that would quell the cravings she'd been having for meat. It was the baby who wanted it. She'd read how a growing foetus needs animal protein. She'd resorted to secretly eating the leftovers of Edna's Salisbury steak TV dinners. She told herself she was eating mostly the Salisbury stuffing of breadcrumbs and onions with just some morsels of beef thrown in. A filet or a New York steak would have tasted more satisfying, but Luna couldn't bring herself to buy a slab of raw meat. After Luna ate the leftovers, she waited anxiously for signs of aggression in her behaviour.

Mark ordered a twenty-one day, dry-aged rib eye, rare, and a bottle of red wine with a long name and a specific year. "I hope you'll have some. If you like, I'll order a bottle of white to go with your fish."

"Please don't. I'll try some of the red. I'll only take a sip or two."

Mark closed the menu and handed it back to the waiter. "So what do you do for a living?"

Luna had been dreading that question. "I help people heal from negative energy patterns."

"You make money doing that?"

"Of course."

The waiter brought the wine and Mark went through the ritual of smelling the cork and then tasting it. He poured some in her glass and Luna took a tiny sip. "This is very good."

"I'm glad you like it. So do you do that Reiki stuff? Some of my patients have tried that."

"No. Reiki has become very mainstream and lost its

initial power. Everyone and their mother is now a Reiki practitioner. I work with sound and breath and drumming, among other things."

Mark cleared his throat, downed his glass of wine and poured more. "Does that really work? I assume you did your thing with Edna and yet she had to have surgery."

"Healing doesn't always look the way we think it should. I cured someone of cancer, well, a lot of people but the one case is documented."

"By whom?"

"A doctor. Do you want his name?"

"No, no. I believe you."

Sure you do, thought Luna. She felt the familiar twinge of bitterness that came up when someone doubted her gift. She didn't like the feeling and eating meat didn't help. She closed her eyes, took a deep breath, went into a quiet space, reminded herself that everything was perfect even if she didn't understand why.

"Are you okay?"

"Oh, yes. Fine," Luna said. "I love this place. I'd like to live here."

"It is outstanding. Have you ever been married?"

"A long time ago."

"Any children?"

"We weren't married long."

"Me too," Mark said. "Married for a short time and no children, but I always pictured myself with at least two, a boy and a girl. Do you want kids?"

"Oh, yes."

Their dinners came to the table. Luna's scallops were arranged around a tomato and orange salad with a little tart of goat cheese. Mark's steak sat in a little pool of pink-ish blood surrounded by some kind of potato truffle and creamed spinach.

The baby craved a bite of Mark's meat, but Luna wondered how she could possibly be with someone who consumed such a thing on a regular basis. "Do you ever think about the faces that belong to the animals you consume?"

"No. I can't say I have."

"Do you mind if I do a blessing and thank this animal for its sacrifice?"

Mark scanned the room, checked out other diners that might be watching. "Well, what does that involve?"

"We just close our eyes and say a silent prayer to the spirit of the animal. That's all." She reached for his manicured hands. They seemed too small.

"Okay. You look like a blonde angel in the candle-light."

"Thank you." Luna pictured the type of women he usually dated: drinkers who wore too much make-up, desperate for sex and connection. She could tell he liked her eccentricity, at least for an evening, but she could feel his anxiety. His hands started to perspire. She lifted her chin, slit her eyes open and saw him peeking at her.

Luna let go of his hands, opened her eyes and asked if she could have a bite of his steak.

"You're kidding, right?"

"No. For some reason I've been wanting meat lately."

"Really? Be my guest."

Luna reached across the table and cut into the steak. She took a small piece, swallowed it, and asked if she could have more.

"Wow. You really do have a craving. Go ahead. You

know this meat craving can happen with pregnant vegetarian women. Maybe that's it." He laughed.

"That's funny. Have you ever gotten anyone pregnant?"

"Not that I know of."

"What would you do if you knew?"

"If I was younger probably nothing, but now I'd insist on being in the kid's life. I could see myself as a custodial parent. Lately, I've even thought of adopting."

"On your own?"

"Well, yeah. I can offer absolutely everything to a child. I don't need the hassle of marriage just to have kids." He reached for her hand. "Hey, after dessert how about we spend the rest of the night in one of the casitas, like we did last time? We had fun, right?" Somehow, he'd removed one of his high-heeled cowboy boots and his rough-stockinged foot began to rub her leg.

Luna decided to have sex again to see if that might sway her feelings for him and his for her. She knew he was mildly interested but that wasn't enough. When he went down on her, she tried not to look at his high hair. He was good at it, very thorough. She wouldn't mind that on a regular basis, but a gnawing fear had begun to pulsate in her blood. It seemed to be coming from her womb. Her intuition told her the baby was his and that she should never tell him.

XVI

Edna fell asleep soon after they left. She woke at midnight. The decorative comb she'd arranged in her hair for Mark was stabbing her temple. She pulled it out, sat up and decided to play solitaire. Laying the cards out on the bed, she remembered she was alone. She could have a drink. It would help her go back to sleep. All she had to do was make it down the hall to the kitchen without falling. She put the cards on the night table, rolled out of the covers and tried to stand. Luna was right. They should have gotten a walker. Edna had refused. She tried to resist anything that signalled "elderly."

She steadied herself, took small steps, holding onto the footboard of the bed. She wouldn't mind having a cane right now. That'd be better than a walker, much more attractive. She could get a carved one with a gold handle. She'd have to remember to tell Luna. When she got to the hallway, Edna turned the light dimmer all the way up. She faced the wall, put both hands on the nubby linen wallpaper and took tiny sideways steps. Her palms became moist and she hoped her handprints would dry without leaving a trace of her midnight excursion.

It took fifteen minutes to get to the kitchen where

the counters were easier to hold onto. She managed to get a shot glass and bottle of bourbon from the cabinet. She poured one after another, a total of three, and then made her way to the kitchen table to rest before the long haul back to the bedroom. The bourbon relaxed her. She looked out the window. The moon, like a slivered almond, hung low. Edna stood up, steadied herself and shuffled to the back door, opened it and stepped onto the screened porch. The air was slightly humid, a prelude to monsoon season. So much blackness and silence, except for intermittent howls from a lonely dog, crickets, and the sounds of desert insects she didn't know the names of.

Tula came in through the dog door and jumped onto the day bed. Edna lay down with her and covered herself with the red and green afghan Rose had given her for Christmas. As she drifted off to sleep, she imagined Luna and Mark together with the baby, remembered candlelight dinners with Hank at her favourite restaurant in Chicago. What was the name of that place? She'd have to look in the photo album.

At two in the morning, Luna came in through the breezeway and saw Edna on the porch. "Are you all right? What are you doing out here?" Luna sat on the edge of the bed.

"I'm fine dear. I got tired of being in that bedroom. How'd it go? Did he walk you to the door? Kiss you goodnight? I figured there'd be some hanky-panky. What time is it?"

"Around two and yes to your questions but let's get you inside. There's a chill out here."

"I like the breeze. What happened?"

"I can't do it. I know you're disappointed." Luna pulled the afghan over Edna's shoulders.

"Did you tell him?"

"I was going to. He talked about wanting kids but he doesn't want to get married."

"Oh, that's not good."

"He scares me. He'd try to take the baby away and he could do it, no matter how many goddesses and spirits I invoked. In this world, he has all the power. It'd be easy to show I was unfit. I can hear the accusations now; she doesn't believe in doctors or medicine, believes she can heal people, delusional, unsafe environment for a child."

"I see." Edna reached for Luna's hand. "It will be a hardship for you to be alone with the baby. I hate to see you go through that."

"Even if he wanted marriage, I couldn't be myself with him. Our beliefs are too different."

"Well, I guess you'll just have to stay here. You can get rid of that awful trailer."

"Oh, no. I couldn't."

"I insist."

"Would you help me raise the baby?"

"I'd love to, honey, but I'm too old now."

"It would be like having a grandchild."

"I'm not sure how much I could do."

Camilla, the stray cat Luna found to keep scorpions out of the house, came through the dog door and dropped a headless one at Luna's feet.

"Look at that," Edna said. "That means something. Right? Some kind of a message?" With a couple of drinks under my belt, I can see signs too, she thought.

Luna laughed. "What do you think it means?"

"It's obvious. Someone's going to die. Probably me. I hope it's not you, or God forbid, the baby."

"Scorpions have a bad reputation. They remind us of death, but they also signify change, or a good omen. It could be about the baby. Selket, the Egyptian goddess is always shown with a scorpion on her head. She commands the scorpions' poison to be used in reverse for good therapeutic effect, offering protection during childbirth."

"I like that. How do we know for sure what the message means?"

"We don't. We go by intuition and watch for more signs."

"What's that noise?"

"I didn't hear anything."

"My hearing has improved with age. I heard a rustling. There it is again. Someone's out there."

"I think you're right." Luna locked the screen door. "Let's get you inside."

"No. It'll take too long."

"Now I hear it."

Tula jumped from the bed, stood at the door and barked.

"Go inside, call the police and get the gun."

"I'll call but I'm not touching that gun."

"There's a flashlight in the kitchen drawer by the phone. Get the gun. We might need it before the police show up. Think about the baby."

Luna ran into the house, called the police, grabbed the flashlight and found herself running to Edna's bedroom.

Back on the porch, she unlatched the door, held

the gun away from her body, pointed down. "Is it still loaded?" she asked Edna.

"Of course."

Luna and Tula went outside. Tula ran to the rose bushes and barked. Luna followed, shining the flashlight with one hand and holding the gun with the other. No one was there. She began to walk the edges of the backyard. She felt like a soldier securing the perimeter. She'd learned the term from Darryl. It had been his job in the Marines.

At the south end of the windbreaker she saw him. "Joe? What are you doing?"

"I miss you."

"What?" She moved closer to him and he grabbed her ankle, hard. She stumbled and the gun went off, a bullet shot across the yard, hit the trunk of the orange tree with a whacking sound.

"Oh, my God," Luna screamed. "I could have shot you."

"What's happening?" yelled Edna.

"Joe's out here. I almost shot him."

"Are you okay?"

"Fine. I almost shot him!"

A surge of anger flooded Luna's body. She pointed the gun at Joe. "Get up. I could have killed you, hurt my baby or Edna. What's wrong with you? Get in there on the porch and explain yourself."

After a few attempts, Joe finally stood. He was in his underwear.

Luna continued to point the gun at him. "I almost killed you."

"It's okay," Edna said. "You didn't kill anyone."

"It's the meat."

"What?"

"The baby's been craving meat."

"I don't know what you're talking about but before the police come, go to the laundry room and hide the gun in the dryer, in the lint trap."

"It won't fit."

"Yes, it will. I hope those Mormons didn't hear anything. It was only one shot. Sounded just like a car backfiring. Their houses are well insulated so I think we're safe."

Joe sat hunched over on the ottoman. "Could I get some coffee?"

"No. How the hell did you get in the yard?" Edna threw the afghan at him. "Cover yourself."

"I'm not sure. I think I must have climbed over the wall."

"For God's sake. What were you thinking?"

Joe made little snorting sounds. "I missed you. I just wanted to see you again." He pulled out an unfiltered Camel. "Can I get a light?"

"No, you cannot. I'm sorry if I hurt your feelings. I didn't thank you for all your work around here and for keeping me company, but you're drunk. You need to go home. We'll talk tomorrow."

"This feels like my home."

Men called out from the breezeway. "Hello. Police. You called for help. We're coming in." They opened the porch door and showed their badges. "Officers, Monroe and Garcia. You reported a burglary?"

"Oh, I'm so sorry, officers. False alarm. It was our friend Joe here. Too much to drink, passed out in the yard."

"Your name ma'am?"

"Edna Harwood. This is my house."

"Mind if we take a look around?"

"Please do. What are your first names?"

"I'm Manny." He stood legs wide, one hand on his hip, the other hovered over his holster. He said the other officer's name too, but Edna didn't catch it.

"So nice to meet you. I'm a widow. There are no men here to protect us."

"I could do it," said Joe.

"Everything okay inside the house?"

"Oh, yes, fine."

"Maybe we should take a look just in case."

"All right."

Luna, back from the laundry room, sat on the bed stroking Tula's fur, feeling vague cramps in her belly, hoping the men didn't notice her shaking hands. I can't live in a house with a gun, she thought. I'm going to have to do a major ritual to clear myself.

"This is my caregiver, Luna. I'm recovering from surgery."

"Sorry, ma'am. Do you own any firearms?"

"Absolutely not."

"Yeah, in the bedroom," said Joe.

"He's drunk."

Manny and the other patrolman went to the back yard.

"You keep your mouth shut, Joe."

They checked the house and came back to the porch. "Everything seems fine, ma'am. Let's go buddy. We'll give you a ride home."

"Go on, Joe. Go with the officers. Thank you so much. Sorry for the false alarm."

"No problem, ma'am. Better safe than sorry." Their leather boots, belts and holsters squeaked as they walked away with Joe covered in Rose's afghan.

"Thank God they're gone," Edna said. "So much excitement for one night. Let's go out for a nice breakfast."

"It's five o'clock. You're too tired."

"I'm fine. You're the one who's shaken up. Help me change my clothes. We both need some food."

"You really handled those cops well."

"I did, didn't I? I think I used my intuition. We're lucky no one reported hearing a gunshot."

At IHOP they both ordered blueberry pancakes with plenty of butter and maple syrup. Luna resisted ordering a side of sausage.

XVIII

Darryl was napping in a lawn chair in front of his trailer when Luna and Edna pulled into Papago Park. Luna was driving Edna's Cadillac, with the new, smallest model of a U-Haul hitched to the back. It looked like a tiny airplane, "aerodynamically shaped" the guy had said. Edna laughed when she saw it. "Are we driving or flying?" She'd had more energy than usual, building her strength by taking slow, incrementally longer walks with Luna around the Palmer Estates cul-de-sac, as Mormon neighbours peeked at them from behind a slightly drawn curtain or a Venetian blind pulled down with a fingertip. Now, Edna had insisted on coming along to help Luna pack. She'd never been inside a trailer and she wanted to see what it was like.

Luna honked and waved at Darryl.

"Coming up in the world I see," he shouted.

Luna called from the car window, "Just here to pack up my things, like I told you." She veered right onto the dirt road that led to the Yaqui section of the park.

"Who is that? He looks kind of dangerous. What did he mean by coming up in the world?"

"I'm driving a Cadillac. That's Darryl."

"Oh, the other prospect. I'd pass on him. All these roads are dirt. The little driveways aren't even paved."

"Around here paving is a luxury." Luna pulled up to her trailer.

"Oh, this is cute. I like the roundness and the shade of light blue and your car space has asphalt."

"The former renter was in the business."

Luna helped Edna out of the car and into the trailer. Edna inspected the tiny rooms, then settled back in a lumpy armchair.

Luna put on hot water for tea. She rinsed out two mugs. "I haven't been here for so long. Everything is so dusty."

"This isn't bad," Edna said. "I kind of like it. I see why old people buy these. Everything is so close together."

Luna brought Edna her tea and began to reconstruct the flat U-Haul boxes she'd used in her move from Wickenburg, securing the bottoms with two layers of tape. "I think I'll start with books."

"You won't need any household things. You can put all that in the boathouse. What about this furniture?"

"It's all Darryl's."

"I'm glad to hear that."

Luna dusted each book before putting it in a box. She pulled a thick broken-spined hard back off the second shelf. "This is what I need." She sat down and leafed through the pages.

"What's that, dear?"

"A book on rituals. I'm trying to find the right one to clear violence. Most of them are complicated."

"Can't you just take a nice bath or float in the pool and meditate? It's heated you know. There's a raft in the laundry room if you don't know how to float."

Luna didn't want to think about the laundry room. Every time she went in there she had to clear her energy.

"I'd teach you but I'm not in any condition now. You could chant some things. I could be an observer. Is that what you call it?"

"A witness."

"Right. So how about it?"

Luna laughed, turned down the corner of a page and closed the book. "I'll just keep this one out."

"You didn't do anything wrong."

"I pointed a gun at someone."

"Oh, honey, you're human, and if that's the worst thing you do in life you're better than most."

"I guess I'm always trying to be more than that. I don't want to pass on anger or violence to the baby."

"I don't think you have that kind of power. Give my ritual idea a try. I've tried all yours."

"Yes, you have. More tea?"

Darryl came by in his high-heeled cowboy boots. His self-conscious swagger reminded Luna of Mark. They probably had other things in common hidden behind their diverse occupations. Her husband, the pilot, and her boyfriend Bill, the short order cook, were carbon copies of Mark and Darryl. What did that say about her?

None of these men were like her father, who'd loved her and nurtured her gift. A psychologist once told her that she would never choose a man like him. He'd disappeared, left her. She wouldn't put herself through that trauma again, so she attracted men with no potential to cause pain. But Luna didn't believe in psychology. She thought it was an outdated system that put people and their behaviour in homogenized boxes.

Clearly, her husband and Mark didn't care about her

work. Like her mother, they wanted her to be more ordinary. If she went along, there was the assumed promise of financial reward. She was certain Mark would be interested in her as marriage material if she weren't, in his eyes, so strange. Darryl and Bill had helped her with her work—making flyers and picking up road kill coyotes for her rituals, but she knew they expected sex in return and she gave it to them; kept her part of the unspoken bargain. But with Edna, though it looked like a bargain from the outside—care giving in exchange for room and board—their connection was beyond contractual.

"I'd help but my back's acting up." Darryl said.

I'll bet, Edna thought.

"Hey," Darryl said to Edna.

Luna introduced them. Neither made a move to shake the other's hand.

"Charmed," Edna said. "Just out of curiosity, is 'Hey' an acceptable form of greeting these days? I thought hay was for horses."

"Huh?"

"Never mind."

Darryl turned to look at Luna. "You seem different."

That's what Mark had said. Darryl stared at her body. She was just beginning to show, a slight curve to her belly. If you didn't know her you wouldn't guess she was pregnant. Darryl's eyes fixed onto her breasts. His brow furrowed. She could tell he was struggling to remember her body the last time they had sex.

"You have surgery or something?"

"Oh, for God's sake," Edna said.

"Anyway, what you gonna do with that vap?"

"I hadn't thought about it."

"That disabled woman, Kimberly, needs it. She'll buy it from you."

"I'll go over and talk to her."

"Well, she wanted me to handle it."

Kimberly had probably bartered sex with Darryl in exchange for the cooler. "Just give it to her. I'd better sit down for a minute." Luna put her hand on her belly.

"You're overdoing it," Edna said. She nodded to Darryl. "You'd better go."

"Yeah. Sure. Whatever you say. I'll come back later for the vap." He slammed the flimsy screen door on his way out, his expression of annoyance lost in the flat sound of aluminium hitting the doorframe unevenly.

"I hope to God he's not the father," Edna said. "He reminds me of my crazy father, Billy. I bet he lived in a trailer park. It's still hard to believe I came from that. When you feel rested, honey, stack the dishes on this end table and put a box and some newspaper by me. I can pack those up."

"I'll just sit and sip a little more tea. What makes you think Billy lived in a trailer park?"

"They attract odd people who do odd things."

"Like me."

"Oh, honey. You're nothing like Billy."

"No matter how weird he was, it sounds like he had a healing gift and didn't fit in. I relate to that. I'm sure that's why my father disappeared. He felt like a freak. It's genetic. Now he's going to miss out on being a grandfather."

"You know I used to hate all those big dinner parties and group vacations that Hank and everyone else loved.

I thought there was something wrong with me. So I drank to feel comfortable. When I found out about Billy, I figured he was the explanation. I felt kind of relieved. Did you ever try to find your father?"

"I've sent him psychic messages for years and never got a response."

"We could hire a private detective."

"It's too late for that. I feel better now. I'll set you up to pack those dishes."

"I keep meaning to ask if you've seen a doctor yet. Don't go to Mann. I don't like him."

"I'll find someone."

The packing took all day. Luna had to rest in between carrying three or four boxes to the aerodynamic U-Haul. Edna began to feel a chill. She'd forgotten to bring a sweater. Cold desert nights still caught her by surprise. The days were dry and warm, sometimes hot, but just after sunset, the temperature could suddenly drop as much as twenty degrees. Luna helped Edna to the car. She backed the Cadillac out of the driveway, blasted the heater, all vents angled at Edna who couldn't stop shivering.

Before she pulled onto McDowell road, Luna saw Darryl and Kimberly already at the door, his arms wrapped around the evaporative cooler, as she glanced in the rear view mirror for one last look at the little blue trailer.

Christmas day: Five years later

Luna helped Edie put on her new red dress and matching sweater trimmed in pink rhinestones. She insisted on wearing her grandmother's jewelled birthday pin. "Look, Mommy, I sparkle." She wanted to wear the pin everyday; to school and on play dates, but Luna saved it for special occasions. After admiring herself from every angle in the round vanity mirror, Edie sat in the chair by the window where Edna had rocked her to sleep when she was a baby, singing the old southern lullaby, "Mah Lindy Lou." Edna changed the name to Edie Mae. "Honey, did you hear that mockingbird sing last night? Oh Lord, he was singing so sweet in the moonlight. In the old magnolia tree, bustin' his heart with melody. I know he was singin' of you my Edie Mae, Edie Mae …"

Sunlight peeked through the blinds making rectangular shapes over Edie's legs as she rocked and waited for her mother to get dressed for their outing to Sunnyslope Palms. They would hear Steven sing Christmas hymns and Luna, under the guise of massage therapy, would do healing sessions with some of the residents, including Joe who'd moved there four years ago suffering from dementia.

The first Christmas Edna and Luna went to the nursing

home, Luna was six months pregnant. Edna wouldn't take the walker she'd finally agreed to use inside the house. She'd picked out a designer hardwood cane on a website. Luna ordered it in Bordeaux burgundy—and Rose dyed her hair to match the colour. She wore one of her expensive wool suits from Chicago and a mink stole that had been in storage since she moved to Phoenix. Her message to Sunnyslope Palms and Gwen was, "You will not claim me!" When Edna saw the cactus garden decorated with an eight-foot plastic Santa wearing shorts and a tank top she grabbed Luna's arm and said, "Promise me you'll find a way to kill me rather than put me here." Luna would have done anything for Edna and so she promised, though she had no idea how and hoped she wouldn't have to figure it out.

Near the end, Edna began sleeping sixteen and more hours a day. When they walked around the Palmer Estates or just sat in the backyard for fifteen minutes of sun, Luna noticed Edna's skin becoming translucent. She could see through her ears. She looked like a stick of yellow light, as if some kind of chemical was being released in her body. Luna realized there were no more healings to do.

On what would be the last night, Luna drew a lavender oil bath for Edna and helped her into the tub. Edna said the scent reminded her of when she'd been pregnant and Hank had massaged her feet every night with some kind of lotion he'd bought on his own along with a chart that showed all the bones and muscles in the foot. "Sometimes he pressed too hard. But I didn't say anything. It felt like he was talking to the baby."

After her bath, Edna got into bed. Luna stayed with her as she fell asleep. Edna seemed comforted by her own hand resting between her thighs, her soft feet rubbing together under the white cotton sheets that Luna had sun-dried on the clothesline.

Luna put on a hand-painted Hawaiian dress with blue and turquoise waterfalls. She wrapped a red silk shawl around her shoulders. When Edie got a little older, maybe next year, they would take a trip to Hawaii and scatter Hank and Edna's ashes over Honolulu.

Luna heard the low-pitched cooing of mourning doves outside in the rose bushes as Edie called out, "Mommy, hurry up. I want to see the angel sing."

Acknowledgements

At Vine Leaves Press: Jessica Bell, Peter Snell, and Dawn Ius. Linda Davis and Lisbeth Davidow for 10 years of smart, generous readership in our writing group at Funnel Mill café. At Antioch: Leonard Chang, Steve Heller, Alistair McCartney and Carol Potter. Twister Marquiss and *Southwestern American Literature* for publishing the short story, "Edna and Luna." In memoriam: Barbara Deming for her generous award in support of this book. Dante Cuccinello, Sue Hogan, Louretta Walker, and Mary Shuler for their endless encouragement. Daaim Daanish for his "Projector" camaraderie and website wizardry. Special thanks to Judith Taylor for setting me on the path. And for his friendship, F. X. Feeney, who said 40 years ago at CalArts, "You should write that down."

CPSIA information can be obtained
at www.ICGtesting.com
Printed in the USA
LVOW11s0415110117
520515LV00001B/144/P

9 781925 417180